"Marriage is more than dowries and suitability."

"Considerably more," Rick agreed, grinning wickedly at Sancia's hesitant words. "But we seem to be sexually compatible, so I don't think you need worry about that. Besides, it's time I married, and I don't suppose you want to return to that sanctimonious father of yours."

"Oh, no!" Sancia cried, knowing how true his last words were. "But I just can't decide."

"Then perhaps this will make up your mind." Rick swooped, and all his restrained impatience was released in almost savage kisses. Sancia's senses disintegrated.

When he released her, Sancia saw the look of triumph gleaming in his eyes, and she burst out, "If only you loved me!"

"Isn't this enough?" Rick teased, and kissed her again.

No, Sancia thought, yet how could she face life without this man, seemingly the only one capable of igniting her passion?

Elizabeth Ashton, a British writer, has always taken her many readers to exotic faraway places—places that she magically brings to life. Her unforgettable characters and thrilling romantic novels have endeared her to readers around the world.

Books by Elizabeth Ashton

HARLEQUIN ROMANCE

2172—BREEZE FROM THE BOSPHORUS
2179—THE QUESTING HEART
2192—THE GOLDEN GIRL
2200—RENDEZVOUS IN VENICE
2247—THE WILLING HOSTAGE
2256—THE GARDEN OF THE GODS
2300—MOONLIGHT ON THE NILE
2311—THE JOYOUS ADVENTURE
2324—RELUCTANT PARTNERSHIP
2347—THE REKINDLED FLAME
2395—BORROWED PLUMES
2401—SICILIAN SUMMER
2425—SILVER ARROW
2444—REBEL AGAINST LOVE

Don't miss any of our special offers. Write to us at the following address for information on our newest releases.

Harlequin Reader Service
901 Fuhrmann Blvd., P.O. Box 1397, Buffalo, NY 14240
Canadian address: P.O. Box 603,
Fort Erie, Ont. L2A 5X3

Bride
on Approval
Elizabeth Ashton

Harlequin Books

TORONTO • NEW YORK • LONDON
AMSTERDAM • PARIS • SYDNEY • HAMBURG
STOCKHOLM • ATHENS • TOKYO • MILAN

Original hardcover edition published in 1986
by Mills & Boon Limited

ISBN 0-373-02863-6

Harlequin Romance first edition October 1987

CHAPTER ONE

SANCIA EVERARD woke to the pleasant realisation that it was Saturday and she would not have to rush off to work. She could enjoy a leisurely breakfast with her father and she would tell him that she had decided to share a flat with her friend Judith Vincent. She had long wished to free herself from the restrictions of living at home, but had had some qualms about leaving the widowed doctor on his own. But he didn't need her, she assured herself, for Dr Everard was a cold, reserved man who had never shown her any real affection. He wouldn't make many objections, and if he did, she was nearly twenty, so he had no hold over her. Life with Judy, who was a lively extrovert, would be very different from the repressed existence she had endured under her father's roof.

Time I began to live, she told herself as she bathed and dressed in the spring sunshine pouring in through the old-fashioned sash-windows—I've been put upon far too long.

Wearing a heather-mixture sweater and a tartan pleated skirt—Dr Everard disliked his womenfolk to wear trousers—she ran lightly downstairs and into the sombre dining room filled with heavy mahogany furniture. Martha Mann, the ageing housekeeper, was putting the coffee pot on the table and also several personal letters that the receptionist had handed to her, beside the doctor's plate. Sancia noticed that the top one bore an Italian stamp, but she had no premonition that its contents would change her whole life.

5

As they exchanged greetings, the old woman's faded blue eyes ran approvingly over the girl's graceful figure.

'Eh, miss, you're a sight for sore eyes; you grow more like your mother every day, and she was a beauty, whatever else she was.'

Sancia glanced at herself in the mirror over the mantelpiece. It reflected an oval face with straight, delicate features, a riot of copper-gold curls spilling over her shoulders, and slanting green eyes. Compliments from Martha were rare, and this one had been uttered grudgingly. Like her master, she didn't believe in pandering to a girl's vanity, but she was devoted to Sancia, though her bringing-up of the child had been strict, and she was never demonstrative. She was always conscious of the difference in status between them. But she was all the mother Sancia had ever known.

'Do I?' Sancia could not remember her mother. She wondered if the likeness was the reason for her father's unresponsiveness—it pained him to be reminded of his wife. She knew she had been an Italian, for when she was naughty as a child he had always blamed her foreign blood. Her name also, which had caused her such embarrassment at school because it was so unusual that she had changed it to Sandra, was another legacy from the land of her mother's birth.

Dr Everard came in before Martha could make a further comment. He gave them both a curt 'good morning' and frowned at the foreign envelope.

'If you want to open it, I'll excuse you,' Sancia said lightly as they sat down. She was curious about that letter.

'It can wait.'

Martha brought in his bacon and eggs, and Sancia helped herself to toast and marmalade, which brought forth her father's scowl.

'I wish you'd eat a proper breakfast,' he complained. 'Not dieting or anything ridiculous, are you?'

'Oh no, Daddy, but I'm usually pressed for time and I've got out of the way of eating much.'

'You should get up earlier,' he told her.

Sancia had taken a commercial course when she had left school with the idea that she should work as his receptionist-cum-secretary, but by the time she was ready, his present one, Miss Barbara West, had made herself so indispensable that he was reluctant to part with her, so Sancia had got herself a job with an advertising agency. Barbara, she suspected, had become rather more than an employee. Looking at her father's austere, handsome face, it occurred to her that he might be contemplating marrying Barbara; if so, he would be relieved if she went to live with Judy. At the same time she had to stifle a little jealous pang, for she herself had never been able to get near to him.

At last he opened the intriguing letter, drawing out several sheets of thin paper covered with an angular script. He read it through twice, then said abruptly, 'Your mother died several weeks ago.'

Sancia gaped at him. 'But I always thought she *was* dead!'

'Martha and I agreed it was best you should assume so. I didn't want you to have any contact with her. She would have been a bad influence.' The hard, condemnatory voice seemed to drip ice.

'But Daddy,' Sancia felt bewildered, 'she was my mother, didn't she have a right to contact me?' What a difference that would have made to her, to have someone to love and who loved her!

'None whatever,' Dr Everard snapped. 'That was the

stipulation I made when I agreed to a separation—her church didn't allow divorce then. Our marriage was a terrible mistake, Sancia; she loathed the climate, she hated my work. Her idea of a husband was a lap-dog, always there to wait upon her. She was a completely frivolous woman, and I'm afraid her search for amusement included . . . other men!'

Very different from herself, Sancia thought, for she was almost antipathetic towards the opposite sex. The few dates she had accepted had not been a success. Thanks to her puritan-style upbringing she was shy and inhibited, and the obligatory goodnight kisses had repelled her. Afraid there was something lacking in her make-up, she had confided to Judy that she thought she must be frigid, but Judy had ridiculed the idea.

'You haven't met the right man, that's all. When you do, being half Italian, you'll flare up like a volcano!'

Which, Sancia thought, was highly unlikely, nor could she believe she was so combustible.

Now, astonished by her father's revelations, she asked feebly:

'Why ever did you marry her?'

Godfrey Everard smiled wryly. 'A sudden infatuation—she was very lovely. Her mother had married again and her stepfather, who had also married twice, was trying to negotiate a marriage of convenience for her with his grandson, which she resented. As I offered a way of escape, she was ready to fall into my arms.' His hard face softened. 'It happened when I was on holiday in Venice where she was living; that's a magical city, a place to dream. Even a dog could feel romantic there.'

Sancia stared at him in amazement. Could this be her stern, aloof father? He passed his hand over his brow and sighed.

'Never succumb to infatuation, Sancia. It's a trap.' Then, his face hardening, he went on coldly, 'The stepfather died and Lucia went back to her bereaved mother, who, of course, blamed me for everything.' He reached for a piece of toast. 'We didn't communicate, and I've done my best to bring you up to be a respectable, high-principled young woman.'

'Early days yet, Daddy!' The process had been painful.

Dr Everard gave her a bleak look. 'The early days are the important ones.'

And you've tried to make me as cold and unresponsive as you've become, Sancia thought, unable to visualise her father as an ardent suitor. Martha had only partly assuaged her childish longing for affection, and surely there must have been times when Lucia had hankered for her child? There was a streak of vindictiveness in her father which had caused him to cut Lucia completely out of their lives. What she had thought was grief was bitter resentment of her mother's infidelity.

'Haven't you been rather cruel?' she asked reproachfully.

'Cruel to be kind. I couldn't allow you to be exposed to your mother's pernicious influence; physically you resemble her, but I hope I've eradicated any defects of character you may have inherited. This letter is from Lucia's mother—the Contessa, she calls herself. She says she's lonely without Lucia, adding in her theatrical Latin way that she yearns for someone of her blood, which Antonelli's grandson is not, and anyway, although officially he lives with her, he's not often in Venice. She wants you to visit her.'

'I can't, if she's inimical towards you,' Sancia said loyally.

'Apparently all that is to be forgotten,' Dr Everard told

her drily. 'The *palazzo* is a beautiful place; you'll love it.'
He paused and looked at her keenly. 'She might be
inspired to leave it to you.'

'Oh lord, what should I do with a mouldering Venetian
palace?' Sancia asked, laughing. 'Isn't the grandson her
heir?'

'No. The house was bequeathed to her by her first
husband and was to come to Lucia.' He hesitated,
seemed about to say something more, then thought better
of it. 'You'd enjoy a holiday in Venice,' he said finally.

Dancing attendance on a crotchety old woman, Sancia
thought scornfully. She wondered why, after keeping her
apart from her Italian connections for so long, he
suddenly wanted her to go. She didn't take his suggestion
of a possible inheritance seriously. Then his real reason
occurred to her. He was going to marry Barbara and he
wanted her out of the way. He had only hesitated because
he believed he was not free, but now he knew he was.
Barbara was still young enough to give him children, and
hers would have no taint of Italian blood. He had been
unable to love Sancia herself because she was her
mother's daughter, although he had done his duty by her
according to his lights, but if he was planning to foist her
off on an ageing grandmother . . .

'Had you made any plans for your holidays?' he asked
as she said nothing.

'Nothing definite; I was going to spend them with
Judy.' By then, her present flat-mate would have left, and
she meant to spend the time moving in. About to
mention her proposed departure, she was forestalled by
her father, by him suggesting, 'Wouldn't Miss Vincent
like to go with you to Venice?'

'She'd adore it!' That changed the prospect—Venice
with Judy could be fun, and apparently all expenses

would be paid. 'But would the Contessa, or whatever, mind?'

'She's your grandmother,' he reminded her. 'You must call her Nonna.' Far from minding, she wouldn't expect you to travel alone. She has very old-fashioned ideas. Your friend would be accepted as a chaperon.'

Sancia nearly giggled. Judy was far from the conventional picture of a chaperon. She glanced dubiously at her father, for she had an intuition that he was keeping something back.

'May I see the letter?' she enquired.

'No,' he said shortly. 'It contains some private matter, concerning my late wife.' So there was something he didn't want her to know. He went on, looking oddly embarrassed for his ordinarily self-assured aspect. 'Possibly you've noticed my esteem for Miss West.'

'I'm not blind, Daddy. She'll make you a good wife, and really I don't mind.'

But she did. Though she wanted to be independent, her father's house would no longer be her home when Barbara was mistress of it, she would never be able to return to its shelter if things went wrong. The old London house had been her refuge throughout her short life, and in spite of his lack of feeling, her father had represented security. Suddenly she felt bereft and alone.

'Truly you don't mind?' Dr Everard looked relieved.

'Truly. I was going to tell you I'm planning to go and live with Judy; we'll share her flat.'

'I thought something was brewing.' So he was not as obtuse as she had supposed. 'I could wish she was a little less flighty, but I can't expect to choose your friends for you.' (He most certainly couldn't.) 'But have this holiday in Venice first.'

Sancia said jokingly: 'You're not afraid I might take

up with an Italian?'

To her astonishment he replied, quite seriously, 'Mixed marriages often turn out all right. I was unfortunate.' He frowned. 'You haven't—er—formed an attachment, have you?'

'No. To be honest, modern boys don't attract me.'

'It's much better to marry an older man, and one who is established,' Dr Everard said solemnly. 'What says the Bard?

> "Let still the woman take
> An elder than herself; so wears she to him,
> So sways she level in her husband's heart."'

'Maybe, but I'm not a clinging vine,' Sancia returned. 'I'll tell Judy about Venice and I'm sure she'll be thrilled.'

Judy was. Sancia told her about the proposed visit that same afternoon, for her friend was spending the night with her. They were both going to a party, and as the doctor's house was much nearer to their destination, Judy was to change there beforehand and return when it was over. The party was to be fancy dress; Judy arrived, plus a costume that still needed some stitching, and over its flimsy folds Sancia broke her news.

'Wow!' exclaimed Judy. 'Palaces, gondolas, the Rialto and the Grand Canal, all for free! It's too good to be true!'

'Oh, it's true enough, but I'm afraid the old grand-mother may be a bit of a bind!'

'We'll manage her,' Judy said easily. 'I expect she sleeps a lot and probably goes to bed early. Sancie love, help me with these damnable sequins, or I'll never be done in time for this do tonight.'

The party was a very original one, to be held in an empty house belonging to some people called Bradley. It had not yet been sold, and the date being April the thirteenth, Paula Bradley, who had a taste for the macabre, had told them that that was Walpurgis Night, the most important of the four witches' sabbaths, and the empty rooms would be suitably eerie. They were to dress to represent Shakespearean characters, and all were to be masked.

'Though what witches' sabbaths have to do with Shakespeare, I don't know,' Sancia remarked as she diligently sewed sequins on to Judy's Cleopatra costume.

'Well, there's *Macbeth,* and there are plenty of weirdos in *The Tempest.* I guess Paula Bradley wanted to add a touch of culture to the otherwise low proceedings. Are you still determined to go as a boy?'

'Yes, one of the girl-boys, Rosalind or Viola. The costume will be comfortable, and the house may be draughty.'

Judy shook her mop of black hair disparagingly. 'But not glam, dearie. You've got lovely legs, and you'd have made a fantastic Ariel with your hair and slight figure!'

Sancia laughed. 'Far too provocative! I don't want to be pounced upon by all and sundry.'

'What's a party without pouncing?' Judy looked thoughtfully at her friend. 'You're a funny girl, Sancie: when boys show they're attracted you always slap them down if they start pawing you. It's terribly off-putting.'

'I don't want to be pawed,' Sancia said disdainfully.

She knew Judy had no inhibitions—she enjoyed making love. It was part of her warm, generous nature. She was several years older than Sancia and light years older in experience, but her friendship for the younger girl was very genuine.

'But you ought to,' Judy declared, 'you're missing such an awful lot, Sancie. Men are fun.' She broke off a thread. With her black hair and dark eyes, she was very much Shakespeare's idea of the Egyptian queen. 'You won't look a bit sexy, and who's going to fancy you?'

Sancia laughed again. 'That won't worry me.' She didn't care for any of Paula's brash crowd, except Tim, her youngest brother, whom she had met at a disco, but he was just a friend.

Going off at a tangent, Judy demanded, 'This Italian grandson of your grandma's, is he married?'

'I've no idea, but he can't be young if he's Mother's contemporary. Probably stout and balding. Anyway, apparently he's never there. Will you be terribly bored without a man in the house?'

'That won't matter, there'll be plenty outside, and Italians are very forthcoming! Oh, don't worry,' as Sancia looked anxious, 'I'll be the model chaperon in front of your grandma.' She sighed ecstatically. 'Paula's party and a holiday in Venice: life's full of thrills!'

Sancia had hired a green velvet tunic from a theatrical shop, and she bundled up her hair under a beret-style cap. She made a slim, graceful boy. Judy's draperies revealed most of her charms, and she eyed her friend with disapproval.

'Talk about hiding your light under a bushel,' she commented.

In the taxi on their way to the house, Sancia was wondering, as she often had before, if she were abnormal to shrink from the masculine overtures that Judy welcomed so eagerly. She had had a repressed childhood and it might only be that she was inhibited by her father's austerity and Martha's rigid moral code. Perhaps tonight she would meet some exciting type who would break down her rectitude, but she didn't think it likely. She didn't know Paula; their invitations had come through Tim. He was a good-natured, ordinary-looking lad, but although she liked him, he was quite incapable of sweeping her off her feet. She only hoped she wasn't going to be very bored. She didn't go to many parties, and when she did usually felt an outsider—she disliked the loud blare of pop music and the flow of drink. *But* this one had been boosted as something exceptional and she had an unusual sense of anticipation; perhaps she should have dressed more alluringly.

The house showed only chinks of light when they arrived, the shutters being closed over the windows. A red light hung over the front door. They were admitted by an unseen hand while a sepulchral voice from a loudspeaker boomed hollowly: 'Welcome to the Brocken.'

'What's that?' asked Judy, giggling excitedly.

'The mountain where the witches foregather,' Sancia told her.

A figure dressed in hairy combinations with 'Caliban' written across his chest, who, in spite of his mask, Sancia recognised as Tim, took their coats.

'Toilets upstairs on the right,' he said matter-of-factly. 'Go and partake of the witches' brew.'

He ushered them into what had been the original drawing room, a huge, high-ceilinged room. A log fire blazed in an immense grate, psychedelic lights flickered and beat-music throbbed from a concealed source. A large iron cauldron steamed in the middle of the room, and a black-draped figure was ladling out its contents into plastic cups. They were each presented with one, and Sancia nervously swallowed most of hers without realising that it was liberally laced with vodka.

'Have some more?' A small figure dressed as Puck materialised beside her.

'No, thank you.' Her head was swimming.

Then another bizarre figure in robes covered with cabalistic signs (Prospero?) approached with a tray of paper flowers.

'To break the ice and get to know each other,' he explained, as he proceeded to pin a bloom on to each of their chests. 'You will look for the person wearing the replica of your flower, and he will be your partner for the evening.' He paused, and added in an undertone, 'Of course, you can swop him for another if you want to, but,' he raised his voice, 'you will be wise to accept him whom the witches have destined for you.'

'Oh, isn't this fun!' Judy exclaimed as she was adorned with a yellow chrysanthemum. Sancia privately thought it was rather silly, and hoped she had not been allocated to some vacuous youth to whom she would have nothing to say. She wondered vaguely if the pairing was done by chance or if someone had manipulated it. Her flower was a white carnation.

They moved away, looking uncertainly around them, then Judy uttered a squeal and disappeared into the medley, having evidently thought she had espied her partner, though Sancia wondered how she could decipher anything. The flickering lighting was very dim and she seemed to be moving through a crowd of indistinguishable forms, but she supposed she must try to find a white carnation since it was expected of her. She mingled with Othellos, Romeos, grim apparitions from Macbeth, 'the bloody child', the ghost of Banquo in luminous paint—but nowhere a white carnation.

Her bizarre surroundings, the flickering light and the vodka she had unwittingly drunk, began to affect her unpleasantly. She could believe she was moving through some sort of inferno, so that when a tall dark figure swathed in a long black cloak stopped in front of her, she said bemusedly:

'You must be one of the devils who haunt this place.'

He laughed, a throaty, sexy sound. 'Do I look as macabre as all that?'

The voice matched the laugh, deep and vibrant, with an intonation she couldn't place. Welsh? Scottish?

'You might be Lucifer's self,' she told him.

'I feel flattered, but devil or not, you're my victim for the night.'

Then she saw he was wearing something white. She stared at him in mute wonder, her senses bemused. Tall, dark—that was all she could see, but certainly not a vacuous youth. Had Fate for once been kind? She glanced up at him apprehensively, for there was something menacing about him that she couldn't define. He was masked, as she was, and she could not distinguish any details in the flickering light; he was just a dark shape, his chin level with her head.

Instinctively she drew back, saying feebly: 'But I don't know who you are.'

'Why, Hamlet, of course. Don't you recognise the sable habit? And you are?'

'Viola.'

'Ah, yes, the girl who pined for that feeble Duke.'

'Why do you call him that?'

She spoke at random, not in the least interested in the lovesick Orsino, but disturbed by this man's virile magnetism. He had to stand very close to her to catch what she was saying, and she was aware of his proximity in every tingling nerve. Perversely, now that she had at last met a man who could affect her, she wanted to run away. She glanced round seeking a refuge. At the other end of the room, those who were not impeded by their costumes were dancing, writhing their hips and torsos in time to the jungle beat. Couples were whispering in corners and the witches' brew was being liberally dispensed to a waiting queue. There was nowhere to hide.

In answer to her question, he told her:

'Because he sent his page to do his wooing.'

'But the lady wouldn't admit him.'

'That shouldn't have deterred him. He was lacking in resource. That his inamorata fell for his page instead of himself served him right.'

Yes, Sancia thought vaguely, neither locks nor bars would have kept you out. Then she wondered what they were talking about . . . the plot of a play she had studied at school, as apparently he had also? What had that to do with their present situation, except to reveal his arrogant disposition? She could see the glitter of his eyes through his mask; he seemed to be studying her intently. A gleam of light showed a glint of white on his chest. Presumably it was a white carnation.

As she remained silent, slightly bemused, he went on: 'Our hostess's ideas of décor for a party are certainly fantastic, but there doesn't seem to be anywhere to sit except on the floor. What would you like to do? Dance? Explore? Perhaps you would like some more of the witches' brew?'

'Oh, no, thank you,' refused Sancia hurriedly.

Of course, that was what was having this peculiar effect upon her. It couldn't be the presence of this man who was a complete stranger to her. Her pulses were leaping and the blood was flowing quickly through her veins. Whatever it was, it was most disconcerting. She wondered vaguely if Tim had finished his doorman's duties, and whether she could locate him. He was normal and sane and would protect her ... Protect her? From what?

Conscious only of a desire to flee from the dark, dominant personality looming over her, Sancia turned away and took a tentative step towards the door. Instantly a hand clamped on her shoulder.

'You're not trying to escape me, are you?' Now his voice was mocking. 'That isn't playing the game.'

'Of course I'm not,' she lied, then, striving to speak calmly and rationally, she went on: 'But don't you think this flower business was a stupid idea? I'm sure you'd prefer a more glamorous—er—victim than I am!'

He laughed. 'I wouldn't dare to try to evade the fate prescribed for me,' he said firmly. 'And neither must you.'

Her imagination must be playing tricks, for he seemed to be putting far more significance into his words than a party game justified. The restraining hand on her shoulder seemed to burn through the velvet of her tunic. She could almost believe he *was* Lucifer or some such being, so powerful was the atmosphere of that weird room.

'You sound as though I were a dose of medicine,' she said crossly, trying to combat her fantasies.

'That's not a very romantic thing to say.'

'I'm not at all romantically minded ...' But her words were lost as a blast of sound swept through the room—someone had turned the amplifiers up. Her companion dropped his hand from her shoulder with a muttered expletive.

'What a hell of a din!'

Which was of course appropriate to their surroundings. The beat seemed to echo in Sancia's brain as her companion hissed in her ear, 'Let's find some place else.'

'Oh no!' she cried in protest, visions of the empty rooms above them and the miles of winding corridors flashing through her brain. To be lost in them with this. . . this. . . what was he?

But, not heeding her protest, he swooped forward, a strong arm encircling her waist. Enveloped in his swirling cloak, she was propelled towards a distant door at the further end of the room. He was too strong to be resisted and, taken by surprise, Sancia didn't try. The door opened on to a passage that went past the lighted doorway of the dining room where hired caterers were setting out the supper on trestle tables, then into Stygian gloom, and thence through another door into what appeared to be a large conservatory lit by strings of coloured lights, faintly illuminating the exotic shapes of tropical plants. The glass roof was far above their heads, and it accommodated a palm tree among other vegetation, its fronds shutting out the night sky. Though the house was empty, someone must tend the plants, because they looked healthy. There was a smell of damp earth and other more pungent scents Sancia could not identify. By now she had lost all sense of reality, and had Aladdin's genie suddenly appeared to obey their commands, she would not have been surprised.

Then, at last, the compelling grasp of her waist was relaxed, her escort dumped her down on a wooden seat beneath a banana tree, and divesting himself of his cloak, which he threw over the back of it, he seated himself beside her, remarking casually: 'Now at last we can talk in peace.'

CHAPTER TWO

THE faint radiance from the fairy lights was no more
revealing than the illumination in the reception room.
Here and there a gleam picked out an object: a green leaf,
the petals of a flower, and the glint of the white emblem
on Hamlet's chest. The distant beat music was merely a
vibration. Sancia and her companion might have been
alone on a desert island, which the palm tree suggested,
and their isolation made her feel slightly uneasy. Her
body could still feel the impress of his compelling arm,
but her surroundings had the unreality of a dream; she
seemed to have been whirled into an enchanted place.
Striving to return to normality, she said prosaically: 'You
seem to know this house very well.'

'I've been over it before,' he explained. 'Bradley asked
my opinion about the possibility of turning it into flats. It
could be done, but it would cost a packet.'

So he knew the Bradleys—that gave him some sort of
identity. The seat they were sitting on was not very long
and he was very close to her, their thighs almost
touching. To ease his position he had put one arm along
the back of it, and she had only to lean back to be
encircled by it. She became intensely conscious of his
proximity. An odour of bay rum and after-shave mingled
with something else exuded from him, affecting her
sensually. She spoke again, almost at random.

'Are you an architect?'

'Not professionally, but I'm interested in old buildings. This house is Victorian, and very solid. They didn't

stint materials in those days.'

He shifted his position and his thigh touched hers, the contact setting her nerves jangling. Instantly he moved it away, as he went on, 'Now tell me all about yourself.'

He could make the most ordinary question sound beguiling, and, anxious to break the sensuous spell that seemed to be engulfing her, Sancia hurried into speech.

'There isn't much to tell. My father is an eminent physician, my mother . . . dead. I'm living at home at present, and I work in an advertising office. That's all.'

'The bald facts, but what about your thoughts and feelings? No affairs of the heart?'

'Those are not matters I discuss with strangers,' she said primly.

'But love and romance are the most absorbing topics for a young girl. How can we progress in intimacy unless we discuss them?' The deep, charming voice held a faintly derisory note, and she suspected that he had not much use for either himself.

'So that you can laugh at me?' she reproached him. 'We haven't known each other long enough to be intimate.'

'Time has nothing to do with it,' he told her. 'Let me hazard a guess. Has some unfeeling wretch let you down and you're nursing a broken heart, hence your reticence?'

Lightly spoken, and yet she was intuitively aware of some purpose behind his questioning, though what it could be she couldn't imagine.

'Oh, nothing like that,' she declared with a laugh. 'Actually I've never been in love, and I don't want to be.' Her parents had been in love, and how disastrously that had ended, as she had learned that morning!

'Rubbish. Every young girl wants to fall in love, if not with a person, with love itself.'

'You seem to think you know a lot about young girls,' she retorted tartly.

'I do,' he said simply.

Even in that faint light she could discern the glitter of his eyes behind his mask, and his regard had never left her face during this exchange. He seemed to be assessing her, possibly wondering what he had picked up, and how she would respond if he made a pass at her, for she was fairly certain he hadn't brought her to this secluded spot merely to talk. If he did, he would be disappointed and leave her for more sophisticated prey. For a fleeting moment she regretted that she had not chosen a more alluring costume for the thought of being kissed by him was oddly exciting, then her habitual reserve took over. She couldn't give the reciprocation he expected, and she never had liked amorous kisses; besides, she was a little scared of this strange being beside her: there was something reptilian about those gleaming eyes which fascinated while they repelled, like the stare of a snake. Made uneasy by his scrutiny, she rushed into speech.

'Do you go to the theatre? You seem to know your Shakespeare very well. I don't often go . . .'

His arm dropped across her shoulders as he interrupted her.

'Easy now, you don't have to make conversation; in fact, in a situation like this it's a waste of time.'

It was coming now—the dark masked face was only inches from her own, and her heart accelerated with fearful anticipation; she was not sure if she were attracted or repelled. She said quickly, 'Please take your arm away. I don't like being touched.'

'Isn't amorous dalliance expected at this sort of do? The jungle beat, the vodka, the subdued lighting are all designed to promote it.'

'Maybe.' His closeness, the arm about her shoulders affected her strangely. Shivers were running up and down her spine. 'But . . . but . . . I'm not that sort of girl.'

'Not . . . permissive?' A whisper in her ear.

'No!' she cried violently. Then, calming herself with an effort, 'Please get this straight. I'm not a . . . a flirt. I shan't mind if you go and look for a more willing partner.'

To her relief he removed his arm and drew back to he edge of the seat. To her surprise he made no move to leave her; rather he seemed pleased by her rebuff.

'Not very old, are you, my dear?' he asked gently.

'I'm nearly twenty,' Sancia told him indignantly.

'Is that so? And still innocent?'

'Now you're being insulting.'

'Merely curious. It's so unusual in this day and age.'

As she tried to think of a scathing retort, her eye was caught by the white emblem on his tunic and she suddenly realised it was not a flower at all but an ivory medallion suspended from a chain about his neck. She put out a tentative hand to pick it up and saw that it was shaped like a human skull. She dropped it hastily with a shudder.

'Poor Yorick's skull,' he was grinning. 'It helps to identify the character I'm representing, and gives the right macabre touch.'

'It does that! I thought it was a white carnation.' Then it hit her. 'You cheated!'

'All's fair in love and war,' he drawled, 'and tonight's orgy is a bit of both.'

War between her conflicting feelings, true enough, but love . . . 'Why on earth did you pick on me?' she demanded.

'I liked your legs.'

Involuntarily she glanced down, but their shape was lost in the shadows on the ground.

'That doesn't seem to be a very adequate reason.' Then the enormity of his action struck her. 'It's too bad of you—we must go at once. Some poor lad must be searching for me—I mean the carnation—and you weren't meant for me!'

But she didn't move. Some agency outside herself kept her glued to her seat.

'Don't be so sure of that,' he said significantly. 'As for your partner, he'll have consoled himself with someone else long ago. For myself, I'm quite content with what I've got.'

'Even though I'm an icicle?"

'Icicles can be melted.'

'Not this one,' she said firmly. Then, voicing her dread, 'I . . . I'm frigid.'

He laughed, seemingly very much amused.

'I think not, merely unawakened.'

'I'm not the Sleeping Beauty!' she began, and stopped, overcome with embarrassment, remembering how that princess had been woken.

'Perhaps it would take more than a single kiss to turn you on,' he said meditatively. 'But once aroused you might be quite something.'

'Thank you, but I prefer to remain as I am,' she returned coldly, which wasn't true. She very much wanted to experience what Judy enjoyed so much, to break through the walls of inhibition that had been built around her by the restrictions that had been imposed upon her. Her friend had told her that she needed to meet the right man, but this mocking, unscrupulous Prince of Denmark could not be he. She had had her adolescent dreams of love, although she had never met anyone who personified her romantic imaginings. Her ideal lover was a combination of Sir Lancelot and King Arthur, with the fire of the former and the integrity of the latter.

She glanced nervously at her companion, but he seemed to have lost interest in her, for at last he had removed his searching gaze and had turned his head away. She could just discern its outline, and noticed that it was very well shaped and was covered with thick dark hair. She hoped she had convinced him that she was not available, and expected him to make an apology and leave her to search for someone who was, as she had already suggested. To her surprise she felt a faint regret. At least he was stimulating company.

But he made no move to go. Instead he asked casually, 'Mind if I smoke?'

'Not at all. Please do.'

He produced a packet of cheroots and a lighter from somewhere about his person, remarking apologetically, 'I'm afraid I've no cigarettes to offer you.'

'Thank you, but I don't smoke.'

His next action caught her completely off guard. Returning the cheroots to where they came from, he turned towards her, flicking on the lighter, with a quick movement he whisked her mask away, holding up the lighter to illuminate her face.

'Oh, no,' she cried, snatching at it, 'you mustn't do that!' She tried to blow it out, and the flame flared sideways as he moved it beyond her reach.

'And you mustn't do that,' he reproved her. 'You'll set something alight.'

Dropping her mask, he pulled the cap from her head and her hair fell tumbling about her neck, the light picking out gleams of russet gold among its strands.

'*Bella*,' he murmured with appreciation, and with his

free hand he stroked the shining tresses.

Sancia was too incensed to notice that he had used a foreign word. Pulling her hair away from those marauding fingers, her green eyes sparkling, she exclaimed fiercely, 'How dare you? You're behaving abominably! First of all you cheat, then you tear off my mask without a by-your-leave ...' She checked herself as a thought struck her. She very much wanted to see *his* face. 'But I'll forgive you,' she went on sweetly, 'if you'll remove yours. That's only fair.'

'Sorry, but I prefer to forgo your forgiveness and retain my disguise,' he returned infuriatingly. He moved the lighter back and forth while he studied each of her features in turn by its tiny flame, her wide angry eyes, her lovely mouth and the delicately moulded nose and chin. 'You should have dressed as Titania, then you could have displayed that beautiful hair instead of hiding it under that ugly cap.' He snapped off the light. 'There's fire under your ice, as you demonstrated by your passionate anger. It only needs to be ignited.' He dropped the lighter back into his pocket. 'Shall I prove it to you?'

'Oh, no, please don't!' Sancia cried in alarm. He had spoken quite casually, but she sensed the intention behind his words. 'This has gone far enough. I'll wish you goodnight, Prince of Denmark.'

She sprang to her feet, but she wasn't quite quick enough. He caught her round the waist with a hand on either side of it, and pulled her back beside him.

'Let me go!' She fought desperately to free herself, but he held her in a steel clamp, and she realised how strong he must be. Unfamiliar sensations stirred within her which scared her more than this forcible detention.

'When you promise not to run away,' he told her, smiling at her ineffectual effort to esapce. 'Good God, girl, what a sylph you are! I could break you between my two hands.'

They almost spanned her waist, and she was having difficulty in breathing, though not only because of his iron grip.

'You're a brute, you're hurting me!' she gasped, her every nerve quivering.

He laughed. 'Most women enjoy a little brutality,' he told her callously.

'I'm certainly not one of them!'

He relaxed his hold, but did not release her, as he enquired, 'Do you really find my touch repellent?'

'I think you're horrible!'

'You've given a fine display of outraged virginity, but you don't really mean that, you know.' He pressed her sides gently. 'Nor do I believe I repel you.'

'Very sure of yourself, aren't you?' she told him, but she ceased to struggle. 'I suppose most girls like this sort of treatment, but I . . .' Her voice trailed away as she realised she had felt more alive in this man's company than she had ever done before.

Again he laughed, and as he released her, he said carelessly, 'You needn't get in such a state. I thought the icicle pose was only an act—playing hard to get, I believe it's called—but it seems to be genuine.'

He again took out his cheroots and this time he lit one. As the flame flared, Sancia glimpsed a strong chin below a handsome mouth. The aroma of the tobacco mingled with the scent of some pungent tropical plant, producing an exotic atmosphere. A curl of smoke ascended to the glass roof far above them, below which the coloured lights shone like stars. He seemed to have withdrawn from her, and inconsistently, Sancia regretted that she had repulsed him. She had not been repelled by his touch; it had excited her. Hitherto she had been quite indifferent to masculine caresses, but it wasn't only anger that she had felt when he had held her. If he were to kiss her . . . her pulses quickened at the thought . . . perhaps for once she could respond. Impelled by an instinct so strong it overcame her reserve, she began faintly, 'If you'd like to kiss me . . .' and stopped, appalled by her own boldness.

He turned to her and she sensed his mocking smile.

'So the icicle is beginning to melt after all.'

'That's it,' she blurted out. 'I don't want to be an icicle! It's how I'm made.'

'You're only suffering from repression.'

She was quite unprepared for his next action. Throwing down the half-smoked cheroot, and putting his foot upon it, he moved his hand to the neck of her tunic. Undoing the clasps, he pulled it apart, exposing her neck and the upper half of her slight bosom. Her flesh gleamed palely in the faint light, and he drew his fingers caressingly over her skin.

'Small but perfect,' he murmured. 'How much more enticing is the bud than the full-blown bloom.'

Sancia sat as if mesmerised, a flood of sensation drowning her faint protest. He slid his hands under her tunic to grasp her bare shoulders, and bent his head to set his lips on the base of her throat, and she trembled, feeling fire course through her veins. As he continued to caress her with hands and lips, her whole being surged towards him, but he still hadn't kissed her lips. He said softly, sensuously in her ear, 'To initiate you might be . . . interesting.'

Her cheek touched the cold ivory of the skull.

That, and the meaning of what he had just said, acted like a cold douche upon her rising passion. She wasn't ready for that yet, she knew, but more than that was the sudden stab of intuition that although he was arousing her, making her feel as she had never felt before, he himself was not emotionally involved. He was deliberately using a very practised technique to test her reactions; he was merely curious, and her instantaneous response was amusing him. And she had asked for it!

Flushing with shame, she dragged herself violently away from him exclaiming, 'I won't allow you to experiment with me!'

He let her go without making any attempt to restrain her. Hastily Sancia refastened her tunic with trembling fingers, somewhat dashed that he had not persisted.

'Could you resist me?' he asked indolently.

Instead of a vigorous affirmative, Sancia, to her own astonishment, told him, 'Not if you loved me.'

He appeared to be startled by this naïve confession, then he laughed, and said indulgently, 'Surely you're old enough not to confuse love with sex? They're separate things, and only the very young get them mixed.'

That was all it was, of course, a sexual impulse on both sides, but Sancia was shaken: she did equate love with sex, for she believed—naïvely she supposed—that the supreme act could only be justified by love. She was reminded that her companion was obviously a cynical man of the world, who was finding her unsophistication diverting. She was thankful that the darkness concealed her flaming cheeks as she said stiffly, 'Of course I know that.'

'Now don't freeze up again,' he was gently mocking. 'You were thawing nicely when you suddenly took fright.'

'It was that thing on your chest,' she explained inadequately. 'I ... I touched it.'

He held up the skull.

'Alas, poor Yorick, a reminder that all things end in dust. All the more reason why we should make the most of life while we have it. He dropped it, and went on: 'I haven't properly kissed you yet; that may complete the process.'

'Oh, please . . .' Sancia shrank away from him as he reached for her.

'What's the matter? It won't hurt. I don't believe you've ever been thoroughly kissed.'

Slowly and inexorably he drew her towards him, prolonging the anticipation with sensuous intent, and Sancia felt the first stirrings of desire, a churning in her stomach.

Expectation became an almost physical pain and she was incapable of any resistance; her whole being yearned towards the shadowed face that loomed above hers.

'Rick! Why are you hiding here?'

The high-pitched voice cut like a spear of ice through the sensuous spell that enwrapped her, while the beam from a pencil torch wavered in the gloom. Bemused, Sancia could only stare, but her companion acted with commendable speed. In one swift movement he was on his feet, the cloak snatched from the seat and draped about his shoulders, standing between Sancia and the intruder and concealing her from sight.

'Did you want me, Paula?' he asked serenely.

'Of course I did! You promised to help me with the wine for supper. The caterers have gone and I've been looking for you everywhere.'

'I found the conservatory refreshing after the noise and heat in the other rooms,' he returned blandly.

It was obvious that Paula Bradley knew the man she had called Rick so well that no mask could disguise him, from her, and she must have been aware of the character he had chosen to represent, for her costume had been chosen to complement his. Being the hostess, she did not wear a mask, and her long robe, her wild loose hair crowned with a wreath of flowers, depicted the witless Ophelia—the girl Hamlet had professed to love. At that moment she did look mad ... but with rage. Paula was not pretty, but she was tall, deep-breasted and definitely imposing. This party had been her idea, and was being held in her father's house, so she considered she was the most important person present, which made her Hamlet's truancy a great affront. But he seemed quite indifferent to her wrath, even unaware that he had offended.

Paula was peering into the shadows behind him, as she said sharply, 'And I'll bet you weren't alone. Who is that behind you?'

'Viola, the partner I drew in your flower lottery,' he returned imperturbably.

'That was a damn stupid idea of Nigel's!' exploded Paula. 'And he hadn't even got the sense to ensure people got the right partners.'

Which betrayed that the raffle had been manipulated.

During this exchange, Sancia had been bundling her hair up under her cap while she contended with an intense feeling of frustration. For the first time in her life she had desired a man's kiss and she had been denied at the very moment of satisfaction. She groped on the floor for her mask, feeling cold and bereft. Paula's torch played on the tall figure between them, but she was in its shadow. The magic had flown; she was in a very ordinary conservatory with an incensed woman and a man who was a philanderer, to whose calculated wiles she had so nearly succumbed. What whim had led him to single her out when he should have been with Paula? She could only suppose that he had guessed her lack of sophistication and thought she would be easy game, a supposition that did nothing to raise her spirits.

The man Paula had called Rick was saying, 'My dear Paula, with your dim lighting and liberal potions of vodka you must expect a little confusion. Viola here mistook my little death's head,' he touched the medallion, 'for a white carnation.'

'Then she must need her eyes testing,' snapped Paula.

'Oh!' Sancia exclaimed indignantly. She had found her mask and put it on. Springing to her feet, she went on, 'You accosted me!'

Paula's torch was directed towards her and she hoped she wasn't looking dishevelled.

'Who the devil are you?' Paula demanded.

Rick intervened. 'She's a young lady who takes a great interest in the works of William Shakespeare. Discovering I had a similar addiction, we became so absorbed in discussing—er—the Bard, that I'm afraid I forgot the time.'

He was leaning negligently against the trunk of the palm tree, his cloak drooping from either shoulder like a bat's wings. In the light of Paula's torch, Sancia could see the amused curl of his lips. Far from being embarrassed, he was enjoying Paula's wrath and her own discomfiture. She would have liked to have hit him.

'Really?' Paula threw him a glance of disbelief. Her suspicious gaze returned to Sancia. 'Do I know you, Miss—er—?'

'I'm a friend of Tim's,' explained Sancia. 'He invited me.'

'Oh, one of his girls,' Paula said contemptuously.

Sancia couldn't claim she was that. There was nothing sentimental between her and Timothy Bradley; he was a little more than a chance acquaintance, and Judy was more his type than she was. But she didn't mind this arrogant stranger being told she had an admirer.

'Timothy!' exclaimed Rick. 'That little twerp!'

'He's a very nice boy,' Sancia defended him.

'Nice.' Infinite scorn in the deep voice.

'Then why aren't you with him?' demanded Paula reasonably. She was obviously wondering what her brother's girl was doing with the man she had marked down for herself.

'Well, when I arrived he was busy——' Sancia began.

'He'll have finished long ago,' Paula interrupted. 'I suggest you join him. He's somewhere out there,' she waved a hand towards a hitherto unnoticed exit on the other side of the conservatory.

'Just a minute.' Rick straightened himself and looked at Sancia. 'For the record, how far have things gone between you and young Bradley?'

Sancia stared at him in astonishment, then she laughed provocatively. 'That's my business,' she told him.

'Oh, do come along, Rick,' cried Paula impatiently. 'Everyone will be coming in to supper.'

'Coming, Viola?'

'No, I'm going to look for Tim,' Sancia told him.

She half hoped he would object, but with a shrug he turned back to Paula. 'Lead on, Ophelia.'

Sancia slipped quietly through the other door. So that was that. He had had his fun with her and now he would look for other distractions. She was conscious of a burning resentment as she stepped into the corridor.

Sancia found herself in another stone-floored passage lit by a low-watt bulb, which struck chill after the warmth of the conservatory. She had no intention of going to look for Tim, who no doubt was holed up with his girl of the moment, but she needed the cloakroom to tidy herself; her hair was slipping down from beneath her cap and her make-up must need attention. The passage would lead somewhere, possibly to a back staircase—in a house this size there must be one—and she could make her way upstairs unobserved.

At the end of the passage was another door which opened into a vast kitchen, lit only by the moon shining through the uncurtained window. It looked eerie in the wan light, a fitting setting for Walpurgis Night; it was not difficult to imagine witches with broomsticks lurking in the shadowy corners. She advanced timidly, wishing she had a torch, and one of the shadows moved. She stifled a scream as a pair of arms closed round her. For one wild moment she thought Rick had pursued her and was about to claim the delayed kiss, but the arms were covered with hair, and the triumphant cry of 'Gotcher!' was uttered in a familiar voice.

'Oh, Tim, how you startled me!' she gasped.

He released her and switched on the light, which she had not thought to do, nor had she known where the switch was.

He turned to stare at her, 'It's Sancia Everard, isn't it? You're not supposed to know my name.'

'You knew mine, and you've taken off your mask and hood. What are you doing in this mausoleum?' She glanced round the huge room, noticing the old-fashioned kitchen range, the enormous cupboards and empty shelves. 'Did anyone ever cook in this place?'

'Oh, yes, but the last tenants installed an electric stove. I came here to cool off, this costume's damned hot. Are you running away from someone?'

'Of course not. I was looking for the back stairs. I—I'm in a bit of a mess.'

'So I see. Was Yorick a bit too rough?'

'Yorick? Oh! How did you know?'

'I saw him sweep you away into the conservatory,' he said wryly.

'It was all the fault of that awful witches' brew,' Sancia excused herself. 'I don't know what came over me!'

'I know what came over him,' Tim grinned wickedly. He had a round, nondescript face, redeemed by his infectious smile. 'You oughtn't to allow yourself to be enticed away by strangers; that one's dangerous.'

'He is,' agreed Sancia fervently. 'Tim, who *is* he? Your sister called him Rick.'

'Yes, his name's Richard, and Paula's nuts about him. Did she catch you with him in the conservatory?'

Sancia giggled. 'She came at the right moment to save my virtue.'

'I think you're a little high,' decided Tim. 'That witches' brew was a bit too potent.'

'I'd say so!' Sancia sobered. 'Have you known this Rick long?'

'My eldest brother was at college with him, but there's a big gap between Carl and me.' The Bradleys were a large and well-spaced-out family. 'He has a business in Lombardy and he's half Italian, and you know what the Iti boys are like.'

'I'm half Italian myself,' Sancia reminded him.

'Good lord, so you are, I'd forgotten. Your name's Italian! I always thought it was Sandra until Judy put me right.'

'They called me that at school. But where are these stairs?'

'Over here.'

He produced a torch, and, turning off the light, led her across the room to a narrow staircase built into the wall.

He shone the torch upwards, saying, 'That's our way. Look out for spiders.' The many cobwebs indicated their presence.

'Your Italian buddy seemed to believe all British girls are permissive,' Sancia remarked as she gingerly started to ascent the stairs.

'Most of them are nowadays, but of course he would pick on you! Like me to go and punch his nose?'

'I don't think you'd make much impression on him,' she told him, for Rick had appeared both taller and broader than Timothy. 'And . . .' with a burst of candour, 'he wasn't altogether to blame. I—I'm afraid I led him on.'

'Good lord, the vodka must have been strong! If you're still feeling that way . . .' He was just behind her and he put a tentative hand on her waist.

'Don't, you'll have us both falling over backwards on these stairs, and I don't like all that stuff you're covered with. Is it tow?'

'Yes, and I don't like it either, but when I've got rid of it . . .'

'The effect's wearing off,' she interrupted hastily.

They had reached the top of the stairs and he indicated the way they should go.

'I was afraid it was too good to be true,' he mourned. 'Why are you always so stand-offish, Sancia?'

'That's the way I'm made.' But she wondered if that were still true. Tim couldn't rouse her, but Rick was different, and she felt herself flush in the darkness. Perhaps it *was* only the delayed effect of the vodka, and in any case Paula seemed to have a prior claim.

'Here we are,' said Tim as they came out on to a lighted landing. 'There's your room, and I'll wait for you here when I've changed, just in case Yorick is lurking.'

'He won't,' she said firmly. 'He's helping Paula. Is she
. . . I mean, are they?'

'That's their business, but I fancy Rick takes them as
they come, and Paula's certainly coming. But I don't
think he's at all smitten.'

An observation that unaccountably delighted Sancia,
though why it should she couldn't imagine. The relations
between Rick and Paula were no concern of hers, and she
would keep him in tow for the rest of the evening.
Meanwhile, Tim was being much more forthcoming
than usual, as if he had suddenly discovered she was
attractive. She would stick close to him for the remainder
of the evening.

'I'll be glad of your escort,' she told him, 'but haven't
you got a partner?'

He shrugged his shoulders. 'She seems to have got lost
in the mêlée. We didn't click; I'd much rather have you.'

Towels and soap had been provided in the bathroom,
and Sancia soon repaired her appearance. Her eyes met
their reflection in the mirror over the basin, which, being
a fixture, had not been removed. They were jade green in
the harsh light, and sparkling. She had made a fool of
herself asking a man to kiss her, a man whom Paula
Bradley regarded as her property, but no great harm was
done: he *hadn't* kissed her, and she would enter the
supper room on Tim's arm, who had already been
designated her boy-friend, which should save her face.

When, once more groomed and immaculate, she came
out, Tim was waiting for her, having changed into a shirt
and slacks, and he told her defiantly that he didn't care
what Paula said, he was going to be comfortable from
now on. He eyed Sancia gloomily.

'I see you've become a cucumber again, and talking of
cucumbers, let's go and eat.'

Sancia looked round the dining room expecting to see Rick, and she wondered what he looked like in full light. He might even have removed his mask, a lot of the guests had, but there was no sign of a tall figure in Hamlet's sable habit. Nor was Paula present. The despised Nigel was pouring out the drinks.

'Gone to earth.' Tim guessed who she was looking for. 'He's a brave man to take on Paula. What'll you have to eat?'

Afterwards they played Murders and other party games, but the evening had gone flat for Sancia, for she did not see Rick again. The taxi came, and Judy was collected protesting from the basement, where she was conducting a lurid flirtation with two men at once. Thus ended Walpurgis Night, as the May Day dawn began to break.

CHAPTER THREE

SANCIA was up next morning by nine o'clock, because her father expected her to preside at breakfast, however late she had been the night before. She left Judy sleeping; there was no need to disturb her.

Dr Everard looked pointedly at Judy's empty place at the table, but made no comment. He informed his daughter that as it was a lovely day and he was not on call, he was going to take Barbara out into the country.

'So you and Miss Vincent will have all day to recover from your dissipated night,' he concluded, noticing with disapproval Sancia's pale face and shadowed eyes. '"Fierce midnights produce famishing morrows", as the poet said.'

'I didn't know you read Swinburne.' Sancia was surprised.

'He was very popular with young men when I was a graduate, but nowadays they prefer porn,' he returned drily. 'But I trust you're not contemplating changing the lilies and languors of virtue for the raptures and roses of vice.'

'Oh, really, Daddy.' Sancia hoped she hadn't blushed. 'What do you think I am?' Thank heaven he could have no idea of what had transpired between her and Rick.

'There, my dear, I was only teasing.' He sighed. 'Youth must be served.' He gave her a sharp look. 'Did you meet anyone interesting at your party last night?'

Again surprised, she told him, 'Only the usual gang, no one you'd find interesting.'

She'd done that beautifully; she hadn't even blushed. Dr Everard would not have approved of Rick. Another keen glance, then, as he carefully folded his table napkin. 'Tonight we'll have a little celebration, if you're not too exhausted. Perhaps Miss Vincent would like to stay for it?'

So he was going to propose to Barbara on this day out and poor Lucia would be finally consigned to oblivion.

'I expect she would, and we'll be ready with our congratulations,' she said demurely.

He laughed with a shade of embarrassment. 'Thank you, my dear.'

Roll on Venice, Sancia thought; she didn't dislike Barbara, but she didn't want a stepmother. She would be glad to get away for a time, while the wedding preparations were discussed.

When Dr Everard had gone, she made fresh coffee and took a tray up to Judy. Her friend lay sprawled in the wide spare bed amidst a tangle of black hair. She opened one eye.

'Oh, my head!' she groaned. 'Sancia, you're an angel. Pour me a strong, black cupful. What a party!'

'It was, wasn't it,' agreed Sancia. This morning she was her usual cool, aloof self, and the episode in the conservatory was as intangible as the memory of a dream.

Martha called up that she was wanted on the phone. Tim, she supposed, since no one else would be calling her. Their acquaintance had ripened considerably last night, but she didn't want to become involved with him. She picked up the receiver and an unforgettable voice enquired, 'Is that you, Viola?'

She nearly dropped it, she had never expected to hear that voice again. Feebly she stammered, 'Oh ... you.

How . . . how are you?'

The mere sound of his voice had made her knees feel weak. She sat down on the hard chair beside the telephone and tried to compose herself.

'As well as can be expected after last night. I rang to ask you to have dinner with me.'

'Me?' She was astonished. Then, remembering all that had occurred, she said coldly, 'Look, Rick, I'm not a trespasser.'

'What the blazes do you mean by that?'

'Paula Bradley.'

'Oh, her!' He dismissed Paula contemptuously. 'Surely you aren't imagining there's anything serious between us? She's far too obvious. I prefer to do the hunting myself.'

'If you're suggesting you're hunting me . . .'

'Certainly not. I respect you. Isn't that what you want?'

'You didn't show me much respect last night,' she said sharply, thinking what a cold word it was.

'Well,' he drawled, and she could sense his lazy smile in his voice, 'that was Walpurgis Night and a wild party.' His tone changed, became brisk and businesslike. 'I needed to know . . . certain things about you, Sancia.'

'You know my name?'

'Tim,' he explained. 'The Bradleys are old friends of mine.'

'You discussed me with Tim?' She wondered when and where, since he had been missing last night.

'He said nothing to your disadvantage, I assure you. He admires you very much, but while I applaud his good taste, I deplore yours.'

'I like Tim,' she declared emphatically.

'Like him by all means, but don't fall in love with him.

He's not the right man for you.'

'Are you setting up a women's advice bureau?' she asked sarcastically, needled by his tone. Who was he to give her advice? 'I can manage my own love affairs.'

'That I very much doubt, but I didn't call you to indulge in a sparring match, but to ask you to dine. We might go some place down by the river, the country is beautiful just now, and you can tell your father I won't keep you out late.'

'Thank you, but I'm of age, and I still don't understand why you've asked me.'

'For the usual reasons. I want to get to know you better, and we have a common bond. You had an Italian mother and I had an English one.'

'I suppose Tim told you that, too! When did you find time to pull me to pieces between you? I only met you last night, and I parted from him at dawn.'

'Sancia, don't prevaricate. All that is unimportant. Will you dine with me tonight?'

Sancia very much wanted to see him again, to discover what he looked like by daylight. Tim had said he was dangerous, but he had spoken half in jest. This Rick had had an English education and an English mother, which were recommendations, and surely the Bradleys, who were most respectable people, wouldn't associate with a reprobate? As for his conduct at the party, no doubt that had been due to the effects of that infernal witches' brew which had also caused her to behave badly.

'It would be lovely,' she said wistfully, 'but tonight is out of the question. My father is getting himself engaged and wants to have a celebration dinner.'

'Indeed,' a peculiar note came into the low, caressing voice, 'he's not wasting any time, is he?'

He couldn't possibly know anything about Lucia and

she returned coldly, 'On the contrary, he's been very patient, he's been without a wife for a long time.'

'And he's missing his matrimonial comforts? Okay, enough said, I can sense you're bristling. I'm aware that Dr Everard is a highly moral character and not a sinner like me, who regards celibacy as an unnecessary imposition.' He laughed, the low, sexy laugh that could so excite her. 'What about next Sunday, then?'

In spite of a reckless impulse urging her to accept, Sancia hesitated. He seemed to be perfectly straight and on the level, he had even implied she should tell her father where she was going, but it wasn't his intention that she mistrusted, it was her own reactions. The mere sound of that sensuous, musical voice vibrated along her nerves, but a voice, however attractive, was not everything. She had not seen him in full light, only masked, and that charming voice might be compensation for a hideous visage, or even a disfigurement. Sancia often reproached herself for her sensitiveness to looks, which she knew were no guarantee of good character, but she was repelled by blemishes. Rick had seen her face, and apparently liked it, but all she had seen of his was a mouth and chin. What of his eyes? The eyes that had glittered through the slits of his mask with that disconcerting stare. Windows of the soul, they had been called; she might find his were small, greedy and untrustworthy, and be revolted. It was only fair to him, she decided, to meet him *vis-à-vis* so she could judge him fairly—which was a nice piece of sophistry, and an excuse to do what she wanted to do.

So finally she yielded to the persuasive voice and he arranged to call for her at her home on Sunday next at a time agreed, for he had hired a car during his visit to England.

'Which is partly business,' he explained, 'my firm does a lot of trade with Britain.'

'What's the name of your firm?' she asked, thinking she might have heard of it.

'Mancelli é Fratelli.'

So that must also be his surname.

Hearing sounds from upstairs that indicated Judy was getting up, and feeling strangely reluctant to let her in on this, Sancia said, 'So that's settled then. I must go now, so I'll say ... *ciao*, isn't it, Mr Mancelli?'

'Mr ...? Oh, yes, of course, but I'm Rick to you, and it is *ciao*. *Arrivederci*.'

During all that week Sancia was in a fever of impatience for her dinner with Richard Mancelli, which would be very different from the dull little meal that followed her father and Barbara's outing. Dr Everard did not care for what he called 'foreign messes', and Martha served them with cold roast beef, salad and apple pie, typical English food. Barbara too was an English type; pink complexion, blue eyes and fair hair. With her engagement ring she had assumed a smug complacency which Sancia found irritating, and her father had a fatuous air as he attended to the wants of his bride-to-be. Sancia kept catching Judy's eye, which was brimming with glee, and she knew she was laughing inwardly at the couple. Sancia was pained that the aloof, dignified father she had always regarded as a superior being should betray such human weakness, and she turned her thoughts to Rick, who, she was sure, would never make a fool of himself over a woman.

Several times during the week she panicked and was on the point of ringing him up to say she had changed her mind, but there were no Mancellis listed in the directory, and she had swung round again before she got to consulting directory enquiries. She said nothing to Judy, shrinking from her probing into her uncertainties, and when her friend asked about her plans for that Sunday night, she merely said she had a date.

'With Tim, I suppose. He's quite a nice boy, but so ordinary. I should have thought you could do better than that.'

Sancia said nothing. If Judy but knew she had, although perhaps she was being unfair to Tim, who was a good, honest lad. But he couldn't compare with Rick, the man of her dreams. For that was what he had become. In imagination she improved upon him, glossing over the more reprehensible aspects of his conduct at the party, and exorcising the—quite unfounded, she assured herself—fear she had experienced, dwelling only upon the pleasurable emotions he had aroused in her. Whatever his motives, he had made her realise she was a woman, and she dared to hope this invitation to dine was a prelude towards a closer relationship,

She bought a new dress, thankful that now she was earning a salary she could choose her own clothes. Yet even the conservative Martha would have approved of what she selected, which was a simple affair in black crêpe that draped her figure becomingly and disguised her lack of curves. Black suited her, emphasising the whiteness of her skin, and the red-gold of her hair. With her colouring she could so easily look theatrical, and she didn't think Rick would appreciate that. With it she wore a white simulated fur wrap, for the evenings were still chilly and it would be cool by the river. She applied very little make-up; too much could be fatal to the demure image she wanted to present. Her hair she swathed round her head, and it was so fine that the neat coils gave no indication of its luxuriance. She had several times considered having it cut, but her father firmly opposed the idea, and she had humoured him as she always did in small matters, leaving opposition for what was really important. A silver belt, silver sandals and a couple of silver bangles completed her ensemble. Round her neck she hung a pendant that had been her mother's, a green stone set in silver. An Irish diamond, it was called, but it was of no great value. It matched her eyes, however, which were shining with eager anticipation.

Her father had been called out and it was Martha's evening off, so when the front door bell chimed she ran down to open it herself.

Her heart was beating fast, almost to suffocation, as she drew back the catch and unfastened the chain. It might not be Rick after all, but she had heard a car draw up and glimpsed it out of the window, long, black and sleek, and she could think of no one else who would drive such a vehicle. It was Rick all right. He looked big and a little formidable in a black leather car coat, which increased his bulk. Black seemed to be his favourite colour. That he was good-looking and unmarred she saw in one swift glance before she shyly lowered her eyes. Dark, slanted eyebrows crossed his broad forehead, their tilt giving him a slightly satanic look; his nose was straight, with a haughty curve to the nostrils, mouth and chin she already knew. A clear olive skin, heritage from his Italian forebears, completed the picture, but it was his eyes that had caused her confusion. Surprisingly they were not dark, but steel grey, their regard as keen and penetrating as a sword thrust. Again she had the impression that he was critically assessing her, as if she were a specimen under a microscope, seeking to discover some flaw in her. Then his glance dropped to her feet, and his fine mouth quirked.

'I am pleased you're wearing a skirt.'

'You don't imagine I'd go out to dinner in jeans?'

He shrugged. 'Some girls do, but *buona sera, signorina.* Now you see me unmasked, I hope you're not disappointed?'

As if he didn't know very well that his appearance could not fail to stir any feminine heart.

Sancia shook her head. 'I'm overwhelmed by your magnificence.'

And indeed he carried his dark head with the pride of a Roman emperor.

'*Dio mio!*' He looked taken aback. 'I didn't expect to have that effect upon you. To return the compliment, you are loveliness personified.'

Now disguises were dispensed with, he had become much more Italian, but his extravagant words grated upon Sancia; they seemed to her to be insincere. Laughing nervously, she returned, 'We seem to have joined a mutual admiration society. Will you come in? I'm afraid my father is out, but I could give you a drink if you'd like one.'

'Thank you, but no, we'd better be getting along, so if you're ready?'

She had noticed his quick frown at her invitation and wondered if she had offended his sense of propriety. Perhaps Italian girls didn't invite men into empty houses? But after what had happened at the party, formality seemed unnecessary. She picked up her silver mesh evening bag, checked that she had her latch key, and stepped outside, slamming the door behind her. Feeling as if she were moving in a dream, she went down the few steps to the pavement, and he handed her into the passenger seat of the car, the touch of his long, brown fingers causing her nerves to tingle. Mechanically she fastened her seat belt as he got in beside her, and she remarked upon the car, for the sake of something to say.

'It's only hired,' he told her as he started the engine. 'At home I drive an Alfa Romeo.'

'Home being Italy, of course. Whereabouts?'

'I live in a hotel in Milano, but I hope to have a house when I marry.'

'So you're engaged?' Sancia was aware of a falling off of temperature in the car, although it was a warm evening. He was only filling in time with Paula and herself until he returned to his fiancée. She thought the Italian girl wouldn't think much of that, but doubtless she knew her countrymen's failings.

'I expect to be if the lady fulfils expectations,' he told her drily.

'What an odd thing to say!' Sancia exclaimed. 'Do you mean if she loves you?'

'That isn't important. Background, compatibility and kindred interests are much more so, and of course she must be virtuous.'

His cool assessment of the qualities he required in his wife roused her indignation.

'You speak as if choosing a wife was like buying a horse,' she declared.

He smiled ironically. 'There is a similarity.'

'Oh, I think you're horrible,' she burst out, 'so . . . so cold-blooded and calculating—but being Italian I suppose you accept arranged marriages, the double standard and all that outdated stuff. It's not fair on the woman!'

Rick laughed with genuine amusement. 'Got it all taped, haven't you, little spitfire, but at your age it's only natural you should have romantic notions about love and marriage. But enough of that . . .' as she started an angry protest '. . . we want to enjoy our evening out, don't we, without arguing about women's rights.'

'Do you consider they've got any?' she demanded. 'Nowadays we claim equal freedom with men.'

'You may claim it, but I mean to make sure my children are my own.'

A blunt statement, but she supposed she had provoked it. She felt sorry for Rick's prospective wife, whoever she was; then, realising that for a second meeting their conversation was becoming too intimate, she began to talk brightly about London and how it compared with Milan, and he followed her lead after giving her a mocking smile. His bride wouldn't have much chance of asserting her rights with this domineering personality, she reflected inwardly, and yet—it would be very exciting to be married to him.

It was an enchanted evening. The rays from the setting sun gilded the buildings of the factory land on the outskirts of London, turning their glass windows to flame. Once in the country, there were spring flowers everywhere, and trees laden with blossom in hedgerows and gardens. The hotel was situated by the river, slow-moving and molten, reflecting the last glory of the sunset, close-mown green lawns stretching down to its banks. Inside all was luxury: thick-pile carpets, floor-length curtains later to be drawn against the night, and deep easy-chairs and couches in the lounge, where Rick took her for pre-dinner drinks and to study the menu. She couldn't make much sense of the elaborate French names and asked Rick to order for her. When their meal was ready they went into the restaurant, which was glittering with glass and silver in the subdued lighting. Each table had its individual candle in an ornate holder and its bouquet of spring flowers, while low music from an unseen source gave a melodious background to low-voiced conversations and the clatter of cutlery.

Sancia ate a starter of sliced pear in a rich sauce, smoked salmon and a main dish of duckling thinly cut, with another delicious sauce, concluding with strawberry meringue. They drank sparkling white wine, followed by Marsala, which, Rick said, was the wine of Sicily.

'A bit better than Paula's witches' brew,' he commented.

Reminded of how that had affected her, Sancia refused to allow him to refill her glass. She didn't know how the evening might develop and she wanted to keep a clear head.

But Rick was the perfect host, courteous and suave, without a trace of the amorousness that had so disturbed her in the conservatory. He might have been a different person. Gone were the sinister overtones which had made Hamlet slightly menacing, and although a little in awe of him still, Sancia no longer felt afraid. For he drew her on to talk about herself, and it all came pouring out. Her repressed childhood, Martha's kind but strict upbringing and her father's lack of affection for her. She didn't complain, merely stated the facts under his skilful questioning.

'I didn't mix well with my schoolmates,' she confessed wryly. 'And not only by reason of my outlandish name. Schoolgirls can be so very silly, and I was out of sympathy with most of them.'

'Your name isn't outlandish, it's pretty, and it's to your credit that you weren't imbued with their foolishness.'

'You're kind to say so, but . . .' She looked a little sadly at her wine glass. 'Somehow I always seemed to be an outsider, possibly because I'd had no real family life and I wasn't encouraged to make friends or bring them home. It was better at commercial college; there I met Judy and she took me under her wing. I was a bit of a prude, I'm afraid, but she gave me a new view of life. Martha's a Calvinist and thinks pleasure is sinful.'

'What a dreadful creed!'

'Of course, you'd think so. You're a bit of a hedonist, aren't you, Mr . . . I mean Rick?'

'*Bene*; I certainly believe in taking the best life has to offer. I enjoy my pleasures and accept reverses when I meet them with, I hope, fortitude.'

Glancing at his forceful chin, Sancia remarked that she didn't suppose he'd met many. 'But I've been talking all about myself,' she went on apologetically. 'Tell me about you.'

He smiled sardonically. 'I lost my parents at an early age and was brought up by my grandfather. He was certainly not a Calvinist.' He laughed. 'Most of my youthful escapades aren't fit for ladies' ears.'

She regarded him solemnly out of wide green eyes. That she could well believe. She wondered how old he was; Carl Bradley was about ten years older than Tim and if he were his contemporary, there must be a great gap of living and experience between him and herself. Yet he had taken her out and seemed interested in her naïve revelations. She was not vain enough to imagine he could fancy her and was at a loss to account for his motive. It could not be seduction, as she had originally feared, for his attitude tonight was more like that of a brother than a lover. Several times she had again caught that look of critical appraisal in his keen grey eyes which made her feel uncomfortable, as if he were assessing the merits of a slave he contemplated buying, but not one he wanted for his bed—his regard was far too cold for that.

'You never knew your mother?' he asked suddenly.

'No. I was led to believe she was dead. I only learned a

week ago that she had died recently. Oh, I wish I had,' she declared passionately. 'I'm sure she was warm and ... and human, and would have given me all the love I missed.'

'Perhaps it's as well you didn't,' he told her cryptically. 'You might have been sadly disillusioned.'

'Why should you say that? Italians love children, don't they? You haven't by any chance heard of my grandmother? She's a Contessa something or other and lives in Venice, but I forget her name.'

'Very lucid,' he commented drily. 'I don't know many Venetians.' He gave her a sharp look. 'You haven't met her?'

'No, but I'm going to.' She told him about the proposed visit to Venice and his face lit up.

'You'll like Italy, it's a beautiful country!' Forthwith he began to describe it to her: the mountains of the north, the sun-baked cities of the south with their dire poverty. Obviously he loved his homeland.

Sancia listened and commented, but was faintly disappointed. Rhapsodies about a country that was as yet unknown to her were not what she had expected. She watched his sensitive hands as he gesticulated to emphasise his words, and remembered the feel of them upon her flesh. The dinner had been excellent, her escort charming but distant. She wanted ... oh, she wasn't sure what, but he was being so impersonal! If she were honest she would have had to admit she would have preferred to have Hamlet back again, whose lovemaking had brought her to life, although she had been frightened by it. But lovemaking seemed to be far from his mind and she felt piqued. Did he, upon closer acquaintance, find her unalluring? Surely her dress, of which he had approved, was more feminine than Viola's tunic and tights? Or had he also been under the influence of the witches' brew? Then she recollected that they were in a public place and he probably did not consider it would be good form to make advances where they could be observed. There was still the drive back in the dark, and their farewell. Her eyes brightened in anticipation of their goodnight kiss, a proceeding she had hitherto regarded with aversion. She lost track of what he was saying as she watched his face, the grey eyes glowing as he described the places he had visited, the great cathedrals of Florence and Milan, the Forum at Rome where the old world met the new. He had travelled all over Italy and was proud of what he had seen, and she wished that *she* could have ignited his emotion, and that his eyes were glowing for love of her and not enthusiasm over scenic glories. But immediately she was overwhelmed with shame, reminding herself that he was practically a stranger and the last thing she wanted was to fall a victim to his Latin lust. Lust—she deliberately repeated the word mentally to check her wild imaginings. It was all this polished man of the world could ever feel for her, a little nonentity whose unsophistication amused him.

He broke off suddenly, arrested, it seemed, by her expression, and she hastily looked away, afraid her eyes were betraying too much.

'Forgive me for boring you,' he said stiffly. 'I allowed my enthusiasm to carry me away.'

'Oh, I wasn't bored, I was most interested,' declared Sancia, not altogether truthfully, 'I only regret I shan't see more of the country. I'm only going to Venice, you know.'

Placated, he told her, 'That will be an excellent start. Shall we have coffee in the lounge?'

There were many well-dressed people in the lounge,

which was more brightly illuminated than the dining-room. Sancia noticed the women's eyes were irresistibly drawn to Rick. Slim of hip, broad of shoulder, his well-tailored clothes fitting him like a skin, he returned their covert glances with a bold stare that annoyed their escorts extremely. He likes women, Sancia thought, and they are like humming birds drawn to nectar. She remembered Tim had said Paula was crazy about him. It wasn't only his dark good looks; he emitted a magnetic charm that nothing feminine could ignore.

The night was lit by a thousand stars in a clear sky as he drove her home, and the air was fragrant with the scent of spring blossoms. They only made occasional banal remarks out of politeness, and Sancia was desperately conscious of his presence beside her in the intimacy of the car, though he seemed to have become withdrawn. He drove fast, for the roads were clear, but with confident expertise. She feared he had been disappointed in her and was anxious to be rid of her as quickly as possible. At last she asked, 'Will you be returning to Italy?'

'Very soon.'

Her heart sank: he would forget her at once.

'Perhaps we'll meet over there,' he suggested.

'That's not very likely.' She hoped her voice hadn't quivered.

'I sometimes go to Venezia.'

'Oh, do you? But I shan't be there very long.'

And Judy would be with her and she would be the guest of an unpredictable old woman who might not approve of men friends.

'Our destinies are entwined, Sancia,' he told her, 'undoubtedly we shall meet again.'

Strange words, and she looked questioningly at his

dimly seen profile, but he did not elucidate and she was too diffident to demand an explanation. Perhaps it was only an Italian version of the English 'Be seeing you', which often meant nothing at all.

At her door, he sprang out of the car and came round to help her to alight. 'I hope you enjoyed your evening,' he said conventionally.

'Rick, it was wonderful,' she asserted. The windows of the house were dark, except for the fan-light over the door. Her father wasn't home and Martha must have gone to bed. Fumbling in her bag for her key, she went on, 'I can't thank you enough, but won't you come in and I'll make some coffee . . .' Her voice trailed away. He stood tall and formidable beside her and quite unresponsive—had her gush displeased him?

'There doesn't seem to be anyone at home,' he remarked, glancing up at the darkened windows.

She asked daringly: 'Does that matter?'

'It does. You're very lovely, Sancia Everard, and I much prefer you as a girl than as a Shakespearean boy— so much so that I would be wise to leave you and say goodnight.'

Sancia's spirits rose; though it might be merely Latin blarney, his words were encouraging.

'In spite of my unattractive garb you were going to kiss me,' she reminded him. 'Don't you want to discover how far the icicle has melted?'

In the light from a street lamp she saw his lips twitch, the fine carved mouth she wanted to feel upon her own. Was this what was meant by desire, an emotion she had never experienced before? Her eyes went to the strong, shapely hands, remembering how they had clasped her body, and her stomach churned.

'That was a sad deprivation,' he admitted, 'but I

daren't make another attempt.'

'You'd dare anything,' she retorted.

He moved restlessly. 'Don't try to provoke me, Sancia. Looking as you do now, you mightn't be able to stop me once I began.'

A confession that delighted her. Was it possible she had the power to move this distinguished stranger beyond his self-control?

'I'm not afraid . . .' she began, but he interrupted her sternly.

'Then you should be. Playing with fire can be dangerous, and I'm not one of your cold-blooded Englishmen.' His voice changed. 'It's time little girls were in bed. Give me your key and I'll open the door for you.'

Mutely Sancia handed him her key, feeling snubbed. The door swung open, disclosing the long passage lit by the hall light. She made one last attempt.

'Rick, you've given me a lovely evening and I'd like to show my appreciation . . .'

He stiffened, and she knew she had blundered.

'I don't buy my women, Sancia.'

Covered with confusion, she stammered, 'I . . . I didn't mean . . .'

'I hope you didn't. Goodnight, Sancia.' He picked up her hand and lightly touched her fingertips with his lips. 'I'm glad you enjoyed the evening. *Ciao.*' He gently pushed her through the door, dropped her latch key on the hall table, and went out, closing it behind him. She heard the car engine start and knew that he was gone. What had gone wrong? Had she put him off by talking to much about herself, exposing her total lack of experience? If only she possessed Judy's sophistication—*she* would not have let him go with a mere kiss on her fingertips. But what had she expected? He had behaved like a courteous gentleman throughout, and surely she hadn't *wanted* him to make a pass at her? Mechanically she rubbed her hand, on which she could still feel the impress of his lips, light though it had been. It should have been her mouth.

Oh, what is happening to me? she thought despairingly as she walked slowly upstairs. I can't have fallen for that Italian philanderer in two encounters. Anyway, it made no difference if she had. It was unlikely that she would ever see him again, for he hadn't suggested another date, only an improbable meeting in Venice.

CHAPTER FOUR

THE excitement of preparing for her Venetian holiday did much to drive Rick out of Sancia's head. Philosophically she accepted that he was an episode that would not—could not—occur again, and now she had time to review it dispassionately, she persuaded herself that she was thankful that it had become a thing of the past. Under his influence she had been taken right out of herself and had acted upon both occasions in an unbecoming manner. She flushed with shame whenever she recalled that twice she had actually invited his kisses; upon the first occasion Paula had intervened, and on the second, he had drawn back, telling her she should be in bed as if she were a precocious child, a snub that made her writhe with humiliation whenever it reccurred to her. She assured herself that she never wanted to see him again, but was unable to stifle a faint regret.

She was on edge all through the period prior to leaving for Venice, half expecting he would ring her up, but no call came, and she realised that he was as ready to forget the interlude as she was, which did nothing to boost her ego. Mercifully, she had not confided in Judy, for she would have found her friend's queries trying. Judy would have been unable to believe that she was not panting to follow up the acquaintance, and would have made wild and impossible suggestions for pursuing it which would have hurt her pride, since Rick appeared to be indifferent. Then she encountered Tim Bradley, who informed her casually that Rick had returned to Italy, much to Paula's pique.

'She was sure she'd get a declaration out of him before he went back,' he told her, 'but he didn't come up to scratch. I guess he'll be back ere long and she'll have another go; she doesn't give up easily.'

By which time Sancia would be beyond his reach, which afforded her some satisfaction.

The two girls arrived at Venice airport on a decidedly chilly May evening, with the sky overcast, which was not at all what they had expected. They had been told they would be met, and waited uneasily outside the airport buildings, gazing at the choppy waters of the lagoon, wondering what they would do if they weren't.

Eventually a young man in jeans and T-shirt approached them enquiring if they were the *signorinas* from Inglaterra. He was very good-looking, dark with regular features and a wide, white smile, though short as most Italians are. When they had identified themselves, he treated Sancia with marked deference as he seized their cases and bade them follow him. Judy he regarded with sly glances which she returned with interest, having evidently placed her in a dependent position and therefore approachable. He conducted them to a motor launch and politely assisted Sancia to step into it, but he squeezed Judy's hand as he rendered her a like service. Their luggage bestowed, he started the engine and they departed in a swirl of spray.

'I didn't realise Venice was an island,' Judy remarked.

Their escort hadn't much English, but he understood her.

'*Si, si, signorina, c'e una strada rialzata*, but him far away.'

The water was pale green, their route marked with large posts stuck in the ground, for in places it was very shallow. Eventually the waterfront of Venice came in sight, the tall red tower of the Campanile, the white façade of the Doges' Palace and the dome of Santa Maria della Salute on the other side of the entrance to the Grand Canal.

'*Ecco Venezia*,' their driver said proudly.

'Just like the pictures of it,' Judy remarked.

'*Non capisco*.' He shook his head.

Sancia laughed. 'You'll have to learn Italian, Judy.'

'Me teach you,' the young man looked at her eagerly, having that much English.

'*Grazie, signor*,' Judy returned, having that much Italian.

'My name is Enrico,' he told her.

'I'll remember.' She gave him a seductive smile.

She's well away, Sancia thought, a little sourly. It had not escaped her notice that as the Contessa's granddaughter, Enrico regarded her as a superior being, and his manner towards her was restrained.

The launch slackened speed as it entered the Grand Canal. Gondolas rocked in its wash and it in turn heaved in the wake of the water buses. The palaces that lined the banks of the canal varied from renovated ones turned into hotels to much dilapidated ones. Enrico pointed out one on the right where Byron had lived and the Rezzonico on the left where the Brownings had lodged, now a museum. Then he drew into a mooring, marked with the familiar barbers' poles that feature in so many pictures of the city, in front of the Casa Antonelli. Four stories high, with tall windows on the first floor opening on to a long balcony, and smaller ones at the other windows, it was coloured a dull red, but both paint and plaster were peeling, as was the case with many others. Enrico helped them to get out on to the wharf, and indicated a flight of stone stairs to the floor above. There a dignified old man awaited them, and after directing Enrico where to take their cases, he told them:

'*La Contessa* wait you,' and flung open double doors into the *salotto*.

The two girls hesitated on the threshold, gazing round the enormous room. There was a scatter of rugs on a vast marble floor, and mirrors hung in tarnished frames on all the walls. The furniture was heavy, dark oak, but in the wide hearth they were chilly enough to rejoice to see a wood fire burning. Chandeliers in Murano glass hung from the high moulded ceiling, and before the fire were shabby but comfortable armchairs and a sofa. The whole room had the air of departed grandeur, sadly outworn. In one of the armchairs was seated Sancia Maria Antonelli, who had once been the Contessa Rossini, and who insisted upon retaining her title. She was dressed entirely in black, and her aquiline face was almost as white as her snowy hair, but her shrewd dark eyes were full of life as she regarded them quizzically.

'Come in, come in,' she cried impatiently, 'I may be a wizened old woman, but I don't bite.' She held out a thin white hand as they advanced diffidently. 'Please excuse me not rising; my arthritis is bad today.' Her English was only faintly accented.

In turn they shook her hand while she scanned Sancia's face eagerly.

'No need to ask which is my granddaughter. *Carissima*, you are my Lucia come again.'

Impulsively Sancia stooped and kissed the withered cheek.

'I'm so glad to be here, Nonna,' she said sincerely.

'It's your home,' the Contessa declared. 'You should have come long ago, but your father is a very obstinate

man, devil take him!' She turned to Judith. 'So good of
you to come, *signorina*; I would not care for my little
Sancia to travel so far alone. What is your name?'

Judith's smile was wry as Sancia introduced them. She
recognised an autocrat when she met one. Later, when
they went to their room to unpack, another large
apartment on the floor above where each had their own
bed, wardrobe and dresser separated by an expanse of
marble floor, she said, 'You'd best look out, my love, or
you won't be able to call your soul your own; she's the sort
that eats grandchildren.'

'I thought she was rather a dear.' Sancia was
unperturbed. 'It means a lot to me, Judy, to meet my
grandmother in my mother's home. I've so few people
belonging to me.' She sighed, wishing Lucia had still
been alive to welcome her also.

'For God's sake don't come over all sentimental!' Judy
laughed. 'I've never yearned after relations myself, and
most of mine disapprove of me. I'd no idea you were born
to the purple, so to speak; this house is like something out
of a film! Are you by any chance in line to inherit it?'

'Oh, no. As I told you, Nonna's second husband left a
surviving grandson and she's sure to leave it to him,
although I shouldn't think he'd want to keep it any more
than I would.'

Nevertheless, when she walked out on to the little
balcony outside their window and looked down at the
vista of the Grand Canal, like a Canaletto picture come
to life, Sancia did feel a pull at her heart. She was half
Italian and the Conte's granddaughter. This *palazzo* was
as much her heritage as the gaunt London house where
she had been reared, and so much more attractive.

As they had arrived in the afternoon, they were
summoned to afternoon tea in the *salotto* where the

Contessa presided over a silver teapot and a bone china tea service.

'I know the English always want their tea,' she said, smiling. 'Lucia had acquired the habit and I find it a very pleasant one. Dinner will be at eight o'clock, and until then you would like to look around, *si*? You must not think I expect you to dance attendance upon me all the time. There is a back entrance from which you can find your way to San Marco square, and old Luigi will give you a key. Or you can go by *vaporetto* from the Rialto Bridge, but perhaps you had better leave that for another day.'

They decided they would, and wound their way through a maze of little streets between tall houses, most of which were dilapidated and hung with the inevitable washing. The way to the Piazza San Marco was marked with arrows, and all the doors to private houses were firmly closed so they looked quite impregnable, but there were many little shops and cafés to brighten their route. The clouds had rolled away and when they finally emerged into the famous square it was lit by pale sunlight. Although it was still early in the season, it was thronged with people, and being surrounded by arcades it offered plenty of shelter if there was a shower. Small, dark pigeons covered it like a cloud and enterprising vendors were selling food for them. Tourists liked to be photographed with the creatures eating out of their hands or perched on their shoulders. There was the impressive façade of the cathedral, the entrance to the palace, and at right angles the *piazzetta*, going down to the lagoon. They went into San Marco, but decided to leave the palace for another day.

For dinner that night Sancia changed into her black dress, of which she thought her grandmother would

approve. Judy wore a scarlet shift, discreetly veiled by a
black shawl. The Contessa wore a black satin dress and a
diamond necklace. She was pleased by their attire.

'I do so dislike modern casualness,' she told them. 'To
come to dinner in trousers and shirts is not right at all.
My grandson always wears a dinner jacket when he dines
with me.'

'Does he come here often?' enquired Judy who didn't
appreciate hen parties. Even if he were stout and
balding, he was a man.

Meanwhile Sancia felt a pang, recalling how she had
told Rick she wouldn't dream of going out with him in
jeans.

'I am pleased to tell you I am expecting him shortly,'
the Contessa smiled. 'It is time you met him, Sancia, and
I hope very much you will find him *simpatico*.'

'I hope so too,' Sancia said politely, thinking that
would be unlikely, 'but he's not a relation, is he?'

'Not by blood, but he's my dear Giovanni's grandson
so he seems like mine also.'

Sancia remembered something else. Dear Giovanni
had wanted him to marry Lucia, and that was why her
mother had eloped with her father, which didn't suggest
he was prepossessing. She glanced dubiously at her
grandmother. Surely she couldn't be thinking of such a
union for herself? Lucia's contemporary would be much
too old for her.

'Then he'll be like a brother to me, an older brother,'
she said pointedly.

The Contessa nodded and smiled but made no
comment.

As Judy had predicted, the old lady retired early in the
care of her maid, leaving them to their own devices, after
suggesting they too must be fatigued and ready for bed.

'A little over two hours by plane is hardly exhausting,' Judy grumbled when they were alone. 'I vote we go and sample the night life, there must be something going on somewhere.'

'Oh, let's leave it for another day,' said Sancia, who *was* feeling exhausted. They went out on to the balcony outside their bedroom, and watched the traffic passing up and down in the dusk. Presently the launch drew into the landing stage, and Enrico sprang out of it. He looked up at the two girls, and Judy kissed her hand to him. He made signs to her to come down, and she asked apologetically:

'Do you mind, Sancia? You said you were tired, but I'm not.'

'Not at all, but ought you to go?'

Judy laughed. 'I'm only the chaperon, it doesn't matter what I do; you being of the blood royal will have to be more circumspect.'

She wrapped her shawl about her shoulders and disappeared. Sancia remained on the balcony and saw Judy emerge and be handed into the launch by her cavalier. She wondered what his status was and whether he had permission to use the launch, but that wasn't her problem. She knew Judy could not exist without a boyfriend, and Enrico seemed fairly innocuous. She watched the launch disappear down the canal a little wistfully. If only Rick would appear and call her down to join him! She lost herself in fantasy, in which she imagined herself drifting over the water, preferably in a gondola, with Rick beside her; he would fit so well into these romantic surroundings, but if he were still in Italy he was at the other side of the country, and she feared he hadn't much use for romance. With a sigh she left the balcony and prepared for bed. She was sound asleep when Judy came in, and a somewhat shame-faced chaperon faced her in the morning over the coffee and croissants that were brought to their room, for their hostess always breakfasted in bed.

'We had a lovely time,' she told her. 'Enrico took me across to the Lido and we did a bit of a pub crawl. He's quite a lad, and I'm learning Italian fast.' She giggled, then looked contrite. 'Sorry to desert you, but you did say you were tired, and your presence would have cast a bit of a blight. To him you're a sort of princess and he wouldn't dare to be himself.'

'I don't mind, and I'm glad you're having fun,' Sancia declared, trying not to feel left out. 'But I hope you're not distracting him from his duties.'

'That's all right. His evenings are free and he's permitted to use the launch when it's not needed.'

Which suggested Sancia wouldn't have much of Judy's company after dinner, and she was still apprehensive about her grandmother's reaction. She need not have been, the Contessa accepted the situation as perfectly natural.

'They will do well together,' she observed. 'That one needs a man and Enrico is a lusty youth.' Nonna was very outspoken. 'It will leave you free to spend your evenings with me. Although I go to bed early I don't sleep, and I will be so happy if you will come and talk to me.'

'That will be lovely,' Sancia feigned enthusiasm at this not very lively prospect, and the old lady's shrewd eyes twinkled.

'But only until Gio comes. Then he will take you out, and he will be a more suitable escort for you than a gondolier, for that is all Enrico is.'

'But I'd much rather be with you,' Sancia protested, alarmed by this prospect. She didn't want to be palmed off on to a strange man who, being Italian, would probably be amorous and she wouldn't know how to cope with him. But he hadn't come yet and might never do so, in spite of the Contessa's certainty.

Her bedroom was next to the *salotto* at the back of the house. There was no view from its windows except the roofs of other houses, but she said it was quieter. It had the same sombre furnishings as the other rooms and the shutters were always closed at night. On the bedside table were framed photographs of her two husbands and one of Lucia, which Sancia regarded curiously. She was very like her mother, though Lucia's face was rounder and her mouth more sensual. As for the two men, Leonardo, Count Rossini, had a thin, sensitive face with dreamy eyes, but Giovanni Antonelli depicted a more forceful character; having obtained the *palazzo* and its mistress, he would have set about making himself master of them both. The bed was a huge four-poster, denuded of its hangings, in which the frail old woman looked lost. It was, she said frankly, the bed she had shared with both her husbands and had been used by generations of Rossinis. In it they had been born and died. Sancia wondered how Giovanni Antonelli had liked using his predecessor's bed, but according to his wife he considered it was a privilege, for the Antonellis were self-made men, not aristocrats, and the Contessa had forfeited her title when she remarried, though she continued to use it.

'*Ecco*, he fell in love with the *palazzo* and its contents and married me to get them,' Nonna said with her infectious chuckle. 'Ours was an arranged marriage—he had money and I had the house—but in the end I loved him as much as I had loved my poor Leonardo. That was a love match, we waited years ... the war and its aftermath took most of his fortune and his health.' She sighed. 'So there was only Lucia when I would have liked a big family.'

Sancia glanced at Giovanni's arrogant pictured face with antagonism. Having contracted a mercenary marriage himself, he would have had no scruples about forcing his stepdaughter into a similar one without regard for her feelings. She felt an inner satisfaction that her mother had thwarted him. A hard, unsympathetic man, she decided, and wondered if his grandson was the same sort.

'You must make a good marriage,' the old woman went on. 'One worthy of your birth, and to a man of substance. You have not, I hope, formed an attachment in England.'

Sancia assured her she had not, then added firmly, 'But before you start matchmaking, Nonna, I must say this. I'll never agree to a marriage of convenience, even to a prince; in fact, I've no wish to marry at all.'

For she was feeling all her old repugnance to intimacy with a man. Only Rick had been able to break through her inhibitions and he had discarded her. Even if she met another who could, she shrank from again experiencing the whirlpool of emotions into which he had thrown her; it had been too devastating.

'Of course you must marry,' her grandmother told her briskly. 'And suitably. Never mind about being in love. I assure you, *mia cara*, it is all the same after a year however you start. Husbands become a habit and it is pleasant to have a man around to take care of you. Leonardo gave me a title and the *palazzo*, Giovanni the money to maintain it, but at his death, except for my jointure which is not adequate, it all went to his grandson. It is your heritage and it is your duty to marry money to renovate it.'

'Oh no!' Sancia exclaimed vehemently. 'That is quite impossible.' She was dismayed by the emphasis in the old woman's voice and mien, suspecting she had sent for her with this aim in view. She went on more gently, unwilling to give offence. 'I'm sorry, Nonna, but the *palazzo* means nothing to me and I couldn't sell myself for its sake, even if,' she smiled wryly, 'anyone wanted to buy me. England is my home where my work and friends are ...' She faltered, for she had few friends and her home was to be taken over by a stepmother. Recovering quickly, she concluded: 'So please don't make any plans for me.'

For a second the Contessa looked furious, her black eyes sparkling irefully. Then her face changed and she sank back on her pillows smiling faintly.

'Ah, youth, youth, so idealistic and so foolish! Remember, *mia cara*, your mother married for love in opposition to our wishes, and what a disaster that was! If she had not run away she could have lived here happily all her days and raised a family instead of being deprived of her only child by that cold-hearted father of yours, and being forced to return to me in disgrace.'

Which was an equally strong argument for not marrying at all, as Sancia hastened to point out.

'Quite wrong.' Nonna shook her white head. 'Marriage and children are fulfilment for a woman, and surely you cannot dislike men?' Sancia flinched. 'But you must choose wisely, *carissima*.'

So far she had had little choice at all, Sancia reflected. She didn't think the Contessa would approve of someone like Tim, good sort though he was. To placate her she said casually: 'Well, I'm still young and maybe the right man will show up eventually. But I'm only here for three weeks, Nonna ...'

'No, no,' her grandmother protested. 'I cannot let you go now, when at last you have come to me. I have not many more years to live, *carissima*, will you not stay to brighten my last days?'

Taken aback, Sancia said hesitantly, 'I ... I had no idea of staying here permanently.' Such an arrangement had never occurred to her. Yet in spite of her denial, the lovely old house was stretching out tendrils to bind her to it, and it was sweet to be wanted by someone.

'Surely you prefer our beautiful Venezia to your dreary London?' Nonna asked persuasively.

'But I couldn't do nothing,' Sancia pointed out, 'I've a job in London, and I like to be independent.'

'If that is how you feel, you could get a position here teaching English. I will arrange it for you, I have many friends and much influence. When Gio comes he will take you about and introduce you to some young people who will be more suitable companions for you than that flighty piece you brought with you.'

Sancia flared up. 'I couldn't have a better friend than Judy.'

'But she seems to prefer Enrico's society to yours,' the Contessa observed slyly.

Again Sancia flinched; she was feeling a little peeved by Judy's desertion. The Contessa knew where to place her barbs. The shrewd eyes watching her crinkled into a smile.

'Let her go home at the appointed time,' her voice was softly wheedling, 'but you will stay, will you not?'

Sancia was tempted, after all what had she to return to? But there was still this Gio to contend with, and she said suddenly, 'Gio, presumably, is your husband's grandson?'

'*Si*, Giovanni the second. Did I tell you his parents

died in an accident? He had no one to turn to but us, poor lamb.'

'But didn't your husband want to marry him to my mother?'

'It would have solved all our problems, but he was much too young for her,' admitted the Contessa. 'The husband should be older than the wife.'

'I don't suppose poor Mother fancied being palmed off on a junior,' Sancia said scornfully, then, as they seemed to be approaching the thorny subject of matrimony again, she hurriedly suggested it was time the old lady went to sleep. 'I will think over what you've proposed,' she promised. 'It . . . it's very good of you to want me to live with you.' There was a quiver in her voice.

'My child, I have hungered for you,' declared the Contessa as Sancia stooped to kiss her, and Sancia nearly capitulated there and then. Nonna looked so frail and lonely in her enormous bed that she had shared with the two husbands she had lost, and it was love shining in her dark eyes as she looked up at the lovely face bending over her. Caution restrained her; she was unsure of her grandmother's motives with regard to Giovanni Antonelli the second. He might turn out to be charming, but she could not rid herself of her preconceived notion that he would prove to be fat and balding, and although she had been told he was too young for Lucia, he could still be middle-aged. Nonna had spoken of an arranged marriage with a man of wealth as Giovanni was, but as Lucia had eloped sooner than be engaged to him it did not sound as if he were attractive.

Sancia already loved her grandmother and she found Italy congenial, but she would strongly resist any attempt to coerce her into a loveless marriage, and if that was what was in the Contessa's mind, she would return to

England with Judith at the end of the three weeks.

Next morning, she and Judith were seated in their négligés beside the open window, when sounds from down below indicated the arrival of a boat, the swirl of water and an engine dying.

Bianca had brought them their breakfast—she was old Luigi's daughter and with her mother and father comprised the domestic staff of the *palazzo*.

'Enrico must have been out early this morning, Judy remarked. 'Perhaps he's been marketing.'

She went out on to the balcony to wave to him and Sancia heard her give a startled exclamation.

'What is it?' she asked.

'We have a visitor,' Judy informed her. 'Can it be the elusive grandson has turned up at last?'

Sancia joined her on the balcony and saw that a smaller, faster boat had been moored beside the Contessa's launch, and the man inside it was throwing out his luggage on to the wharf. Her heart lurched and she clutched at the balustrade as she recognised him, for there was no mistaking that imperious dark head, the low sexy laugh as he said something to Luigi who was assisting him. Then fearful that he would look up and see her watching him she drew back hastily into the bedroom.

'He really is a dish,' remarked Judy, then realising Sancia had gone, followed her inside. 'What's the matter? You look as though you've seen a ghost.'

'I . . . I know who he is,' Sancia faltered. 'I . . . I met him at Paula's party.'

Rick had actually come to call; he must have discovered who her grandmother was, but his coming had thrown her into a turmoil of conflicting emotions. Though in her imagination she had recreated him as a romantic lover, the glimpse of his physical presence had reminded her that he was nothing of the sort and that she was in reality somewhat afraid of him. How was she going to explain him to her grandmother, or to Judy for that matter, who was eyeing her curiously.

'You've kept very quiet about him,' Judy observed. 'Don't tell me you went and got yourself seduced.'

'Oh, don't be absurd!' cried Sancia, blushing hotly. She glanced apprehensively at the door, half expecting Rick to come barging in. Then she recollected where she was, and that Signor Mancelli would have to pay his respects to the Contessa before he asked for her, for this was Italy where a certain amount of formality was still preserved. If the old lady was not up yet, he would be expected to wait until she was ready to receive him. She was torn between a wild desire to flee and a desperate longing to rush downstairs and intercept him.

'Better get dressed,' Judy advised, noting her agitation with amusement. 'Perhaps your cavalier will take us to the Lido. I like the look of his speedboat.'

For that was where they had intended to spend the morning, crossing in the ferry that plied between the town and the island.

Sancia threw off her gown and put on the yellow sundress she had put out to wear. It left her arms and legs bare, which were beautifully tanned after a week of Italian sun. With her copper curls she looked a golden girl, her eyes a vivid green. Reaching for her sandals, she said breathlessly, 'We can't ask him. Let's go . . . now.'

Judy paused in her own toilet to gasp at her, 'But hasn't this guy come to see you?'

'No . . . yes . . . I don't know. I never expected him!'

There was a knock at the door and she started violently. It was only Bianca to tell them the Contessa requested their presence in the *salotto*.

CHAPTER FIVE

THE Venetian blinds were drawn over the windows of the *salotto* to shut out the rays of the sun, which were becoming fierce as the summer advanced. The pale, aqueous light illuminated the tarnished mirrors which reflected an endless succession of tall, dark men so that the entire room seemed impregnated by his presence. He wore a white sleeveless sweater and white trousers, arms and neck burned to the colour of mahogany, and he quite dwarfed the Contessa, whose cheeks were pink with pleasure as she looked up at him with adoring eyes from the depths of her favourite easy chair.

Sancia advanced nervously into the room, finding herself unwilling to encounter his steely penetrating gaze that always disconcerted her. She became very conscious of her bare limbs and wished she was wearing trousers and a shirt, even though, or perhaps perversely because, she knew he didn't like women to wear trousers. Judy, behind her, was barefacedly ogling the new arrival.

The Contessa turned her head towards them, looking ten years younger, her eyes very bright in her flushed face as if she had absorbed some of the intense vitality emanating from the man leaning nonchantly against the mantelpiece.

'Sancia, *mia cara*, may I present *il signor Antonelli*.'

'No, Nonna,' *il signor* protested, 'Not so formal, you'll frighten these charming ladies.' He detached himself from the mantelpiece with easy grace, and, clicking his

76

heels, bowed to them theatrically. 'My English friends call me Rick.'

Bewildered, Sancia looked from him towards her grandmother, who was beaming with love and pride. So this must be Gio; how many names did he go under? she wondered with rising indignation. Each time she met him he assumed a different character.

'Is this another masquerade?' she demanded scornfully. 'You change your colours like a chameleon, *signor*. In London you were Richard Mancelli, when you weren't impersonating the Prince of Denmark!'

He laughed, the deep, sexy laugh that always stirred her.

'Mancelli is the name of my firm, which you mistakenly applied to me. My baptismal names are Giovanni Riccardo Antonelli. Richard being the anglicised form of my middle name, I prefer to use it when I visit your country. Satisfied?'

Nonna glanced from one to the other with mingled astonishment and consternation, sensing something was wrong.

'*Mia cara*, why didn't you tell me you had met Gio?'

'Because I'd no idea that your Gio was the man I met at a masked party,' Sancia told her angrily. 'He took me out and pretended he didn't know you. It seems he delights in mysteries.'

She felt he had made a fool of her, and she was desperately trying to recall what she had said to him over dinner. He had drawn her out very skilfully while keeping his own identity a secret, and probably she had been very indiscreet.

'To meet in disguise is in the best romantic tradition,' Rick returned airily. 'After all, I knew you first as Viola. But what's in a name, as the Bard you admire enquired.'

He smiled at the Contessa. 'Sancia is a student of Shakespeare, Nonna.'

'She is on holiday now,' the old lady, who was not, returned. 'Signorina Vincent,' she never used Judy's first name, 'would you ring for coffee?' Then, recollecting she had not introduced her, went on, 'This is Sancia's friend and companion, Gio.'

'*Come sta*,' Judy smiled, airing her newly acquired Italian.

'*Felice di conoscarla, signorina*,' Rick returned gravely, his eyes dancing with mischief.

'I see you are dressed for the Lido.' The Contessa was frowning at Judy's daring beach pyjamas. 'As I shall retire to recover from the excitement of Gio's arrival, perhaps he will take you there.'

'Delighted,' Rick purred.

'Oh, please don't bother, we were going by water-bus,' Sancia said stiffly.

'But if Signor Antonelli is willing to take us it would be much pleasanter,' Judy interposed, giving him a sexy smile.

Nonna's frown deepened. 'What is the matter, Sancia?' she asked sharply. 'I wish for you and Gio to be friends, but you say you have met already. Has he offended you?' She turned on Rick. 'You bad boy, you knew who she was; did you not treat her with the respect due to my granddaughter?'

Rick's eyes were full of devilish amusement, but he said meekly, 'But of course, Nonna, need you ask?'

If she hadn't been so incensed, Sancia could have laughed at his impudence. Hamlet's behaviour couldn't be described as respectful. Inwardly seething, she couldn't tell him what she thought of his behaviour in front of the old lady, and it was becoming clear to her what his aim had been. Knowing the Contessa was planning a match between them, he had wanted to obtain a prior inspection of his proposed bride without revealing who he was. Now she understood those critical, appraising glances, the reason for his personal questions. He had been weighing her up.

'I don't like deceit,' she said bluntly.

'In what way did I deceive you?' he asked suavely. 'My name? You and your friends don't use surnames, and I do live in Milano.'

'But you never told me you had met her,' Nonna complained.

He turned to her. 'I was going to, when I saw you again. I congratulate you, Nonna upon possessing a very charming granddaughter.'

You won't get round me that way, Sancia thought, as she enquired, 'If you'd found I wasn't—er—presentable, would you have insisted that my visit to Venice was cancelled on some pretext or other?'

Rick called the old lady Nonna though she was not his grandmother, and his hard face softened when he looked at her. Those two loved each other, and Sancia suddenly felt an outsider. Rick had usurped the place she should have filled but for her father's prohibition.

'The Contessa's granddaughter couldn't be anything but presentable,' Rick countered quickly.

Oh, he had a glib tongue, but, recalling his probings about her love life, Sancia began indignantly, 'You wanted to make sure I wasn't like . . .' but stopped in time as she saw an unhappy look cross her grandmother's face; she had nearly said 'my mother'. That would have been a dreadful blunder.

Rick had seen it too, and he threw her a warning look. He seemed about to say something, and she quailed, expecting a scathing comment. But before he could speak, Bianca entered with the coffee. During the business of distributing it, pouring it, sugaring, creaming and handing it round, the atmosphere lightened, but there was an ominous glitter in Rick's eyes whenever he looked at Sancia and she knew he meant to make her pay for her *faux pas* when an opportunity presented itself. Her feelings were chaotic; she was furious with him for the mean trick he had played upon her and was determined to show her displeasure, and yet as he moved about the room her eyes involuntarily followed him, his magnetic personality enchaining her senses. She had dreamed of him, made up fantasies about him, but now she saw him again in the flesh she was part fascinated, part repelled. Had she been less agitated, she would have been amused by Judy's dilemma. He was being charming to her, and Judy's instinct was to annex every male with whom she came in contact, but since Sancia appeared to have a prior claim, loyalty to her friend restrained her. As it was, the prick of jealousy was added to Sancia's emotions—need he be quite so responsive to Judy's coquetry? It was he who said suddenly:

'*Bene*, if you ladies wish to go to the Lido we had better depart before more of the morning has gone.'

'How noble of you to be ready to take us after Sancia's ungraciousness,' exclaimed Judy with a touch of malice.

'Oh, I'm very forgiving,' Rick told her, which Sancia was sure was untrue. 'But three is an awkward number for an outing. Nonna, will you lend us that sexy boatman of yours to make a quartet? I suppose he's somewhere around.'

'Officially helping in the kitchen, but probably flirting with Bianca,' said the Contessa drily. 'But do not give him ideas above his station, Gio.'

'Nonsense, this is a democratic age,' Rick declared lightly. 'Forgive us for deserting you, but you need a rest, you look flushed.' He stooped to kiss her. 'We shan't be long.'

'Do not hurry back on my account,' she bade him, stroking his sleeve. 'Have your *colazione* on the island, and I will see you at dinner.'

While Rick went in search of Enrico, the girls went upstairs to collect their beach bags, and Judy observed, 'You are a dark horse! Fancy meeting a gorgeous guy like that and never letting on.'

'He's devious and mean!' Sancia returned heatedly, still smarting from Rick's deception.

'Don't you like him?'

'I think I hate him.'

'But you'd prefer I kept in the background?'

'Not at all, I'm not keen on Italian philanderers,' Sancia declared. 'You're welcome to him if you can get him!'

'Do you really mean that?'

'Yes,' said Sancia firmly. Judy was confident that where men were concerned Sancia couldn't compete with her, and she received this statement with satisfaction, though she threw Sancia a doubtful look. Sancia was reflecting that if Judy made a conquest of Rick it would scotch her grandmother's matrimonial plans— but this thought was not without a lingering regret.

Rick, with Enrico in tow, met them at the wharf, both men seeming to be in high spirits. There was barely room for the four of them in the speedboat. The two girls sat together on the seat in the stern; Rick was at the controls with Enrico crouched beside him. As soon as they reached the lagoon Rick increased their speed, and the craft fairly bounced over the water, her prow rising

metres above it. Judy shrieked and clutched at the side of
the boat, but Sancia was exhilarated. Once Rick turned
his head and flashed her a smile.

'Enjoying it?' he called.

'It's great,' she laughed back, and knew she had risen
in his estimation. She forgot her grievance and he his
annoyance with her. They were united in the exuberance
induced by their swift progress. How splendid he looks,
she thought, with a stir of her pulses. Rick had discarded
his pullover, and his thin silk shirt was flattened against
his broad chest by the wind of their going, his hair blown
back from his eagle profile as he lifted his face to the sky.

The Lido is a very long and very narrow strip of land,
once covered with dense vegetation prior to the First
World War. Since then it has been developed into a
tourist centre, with hotels, shops and villas. Unlike
Venice, it is thronged with cars and buses brought over
by car ferry. On its southern side are seven kilometres of
sand encrusted with every variety of shell, which has
become one of the best known beaches in the world.

Rounding the western tip of the island, they came
upon it, and Rick steered the boat up to a private wharf
belonging to the Hotel Regina, which rented its own
piece of shore. There an attendant came to intercept
them, and greeted Rick with enthusiasm, for, as he told
them, he was well known at the hotel where they would
lunch.

Sancia was no great swimmer and the water was still
cold. She soon left it to lie in the hot sun under a beach
umbrella, where Judy and Enrico joined her. Rick,
impervious to chill, was only a black head far out in the
lagoon.

'What energy!' Judy exclaimed. 'He swims like a seal!
Enrico, you're being lazy.'

'Me, I likka to be wiz you,' Enrico explained, stroking her arm.

'I could do with a drink,' Judy sighed. 'That boat trip shook me up. Your boss drives it like a maniac.'

'Him notta my boss. Contessa zat,' Enrico corrected her, 'You want drink, we getta.' Since he had known Judy his vocabulary had been much enlarged.

They wandered off, leaving Sancia lying on the sand. Presently Rick came ashore, shaking his wet head as a dog shakes its wet coat. Their towels and wraps were strewn on the sand, and picking up one, he dried himself vigorously while Sancia admired his splendid physique. Like the dozens of bare torsos she had seen on the beaches, his was denuded of hair, either by nature or art, and his bronzed limbs had the smooth perfection of a Greek statue; Apollo or Hermes. He shot a sudden glance at her from under his thick eyelashes and she blushed, saying hastily, 'Was the water cold?'

'I didn't find it so. Where are the others?'

'Judy needed a drink. She didn't appreciate your speedboat.'

He laughed scornfully, 'She was chicken!'

'She's not used to boats,' Sancia defended her. 'I believe you tried to scare us; that wasn't very kind.'

'You weren't frightened, you were exhilarated.'

'Well, I suppose I'm different.'

'I'm glad you are,' he said with meaning. Casting aside the towel, he dropped down on the sand and closed his eyes. Thus Sancia was able to study him unobserved. Physically Rick was a beautiful specimen of manhood, and she had always been susceptible to good looks, but, except for his affection for the Contessa, he seemed hard, and she still resented the way he had approached her at the party without disclosing his identity; devious and calculating, she decided.

She was wearing a swimsuit of unusual design, one half being white, the other black with a red sunburst from one shoulder to the waist. Much less revealing than Judy's bikini, which left little to the imagination, but she had seen Rick look at her friend with distaste, and she recalled what he had said in the conservatory about buds and blossoms. Remembered with a blush the sequel. Was she like her mother after all?

She said suddenly, 'Tell me about my mother, Rick. Didn't your tyrannical grandfather want you to marry her?'

His eyes flew open and he gave her a startled look.

'Good Lord, no! When Lucia was marriageable I was practically an infant. She was ten years older than I.' Sancia calculated quickly: that meant he was in his thirties. 'When she came back several years later, Nonna did suggest we might be able to get her marriage annulled so that we could wed and share the *palazzo*, which she refused to sell to me, saying it must go to Lucia. By then I was about your age, but I persuaded her it wasn't feasible.'

'But weren't you at college?'

'Only for a year—the business was going downhill and I had to come back to take it over.' He smiled wryly. 'The company directors were suspicious of my youth, but I had the controlling interest and I—coped. But about your mother, hasn't Nonna talked about her?'

'Oh, she has.' The Contessa had supplied her with a string of descriptions and anecdotes about Lucia when she was young. 'But she makes out she was a saintly martyr, cast off by my father for a mere indiscretion, etc, etc; I don't think it can be a true picture. Is it right that she took up good works on her return? Nonna says she visited orphanages, things like that.'

Rick sat up abruptly, and said sharply, 'She told you that?'

'Didn't she?'

His tone changed. 'I daresay. I don't know a lot about what she did after I'd gone to Milano. Nonna has built up a myth about her which I've tried to preserve for her sake, but your mother was certainly not saintly.' His eyes went to the distant horizon and a far-off look came into them as he went on softly, 'She was lovely when she was a young girl. I saw her during my school holidays because, as you know, the *palazzo* became my home after my parents died. Physically you're very like her: the same gorgeous hair, and long green eyes—Rossini eyes, they're a characteristic of that family.'

'So when you saw my face in the conservatory you thought I might be like her in other ways?' Sancia asked tartly.

'No, *mia cara*, you'd innocence written all over you.'

'Oh, really!' She was stung. 'You sound as if I were a baby. I do know the facts of life!'

'Theoretically, perhaps, and I did make sure.'

'By half undressing me,' Sancia exclaimed indignantly, 'and . . . and . . .' She felt again his lips upon her neck. 'You behaved abominably!'

His eyes gleamed. 'Don't pretend. You enjoyed it.'

Disturbed by his expression, she said firmly, 'I did not!'

He shrugged his shoulders. 'Have it your own way, but I wouldn't have let you come near Nonna had you been as promiscuous as—many of your friends.'

She noticed the pause—had he been going to say 'your mother'?

'Well, I think my mother had a raw deal,' she declared.

'Losing her own father, being bullied by her stepfather, threatened with an uncongenial marriage . . .'

'The one she made for herself being so successful,' Rick interpolated silkily.

'Well, Daddy did neglect her . . .'

'Exactly. He was quite the wrong man for her. Nonna knew her tendencies; the man he selected would not have neglected her and he would have known how to keep her in order.'

'In what way?'

'Taken a strap to her when necessary.'

'Rick!' Sancia shivered. 'You're joking.'

He again shrugged his shoulders.

'At least Daddy was civilised,' Sancia went on. 'He'd never beat her.'

'That was his mistake. Lucia would have accepted it as an expression of jealous love. She was that sort of woman—any physical violence excited her. The one thing that type can't bear is being taken for granted.'

Sancia stared at him, deeply shocked. 'And you say I'm like her?'

'Only outwardly. You had a Calvinistic upbringing.'

He was smiling, but Sancia was too dismayed to respond.

'But you, Rick,' she enquired, searching his hard, enigmatic face anxiously. 'Would you beat your wife if she was unfaithful?'

'I'd probably strangle her.' Then, seeing her horrified look, he laughed. 'Not having one, I can't say. As you put it, it's uncivilised to lift a hand against a woman, but if I was sufficiently provoked, I might.'

He's capable if it, Sancia thought; he could be cruel. An icy trickle ran down her spine. Underneath his surface charm and veneer lay the violent nature of the

Latin male. A line from Macbeth occurred to her. 'Be bloody, bold and resolute: laugh to scorn the power of man.' Riccardo Antonelli could be all that.

She said vehemently, 'I've never been an advocate of Women's Lib before, but you'll make me a rabid one. Women aren't chattels! My mother had a right to live her own life in her own way, and I don't suppose for one moment your record is lily-white.'

Rick grinned wickedly, which roused her to fury because she didn't realise he had been only half serious. 'It's the same old story, a double standard.' Her eyes flashed. 'Your grandfather, my father and yourself condemning my mother because she wouldn't conform to your outdated ideas, while *you* do as you please!'

'*Bravo, carissima*, what a fine display of rhetoric!' His eyes mocked her. 'But why waste so much passion on abstractions when it could be so much more pleasantly employed?'

Seeing the mischievous gleam in his eyes, Sancia became uneasy.

'I don't know what you mean.'

'Don't you, Sancia?' he asked softly, and her pulses quickened. 'I think you do. Come here.'

'No. I'm going to dress.'

But before she could get to her feet, his hands snaked out and pressed her down on to the sand. Looming over her, he told her with laughter in his voice:

'You owe me a kiss. Twice I've been defrauded by circumstances intervening. May I have it now—and I think some interest must have accrued?'

This reminder of the two occasions upon which she had forgotten herself further enraged her. She glared up into the dark face bending over her.

'Most certainly you may not.'

'Then I'll have to take my due.'

'Don't you dare to try any of your primitive stuff on me!' But her heart was pounding under the pressure of his hands, and although she was unaware of it, her eyes invited.

'I never could resist a challenge.'

She pushed at his hard chest, trying to wriggle free, but he lowered himself so that he was lying half on top of her, his weight imprisoning her so that she could not move. Slowly, sensuously, he began to caress her, stroking her bare limbs, sliding the straps of her costume off her shoulders and drawing his lips over her neck and breasts leaving a trail of fire. He was a past master at the art of arousal, and against her will her body responded to his treatment. Her arms went round his neck, her fingers twining in his thick hair.

'Oh, Rick,' she half sobbed. 'Don't . . . please don't!'

'Want me to stop?'

'Yes . . . no . . .' Her voice faded as his mouth closed over hers. At last he had kissed her lips, a long, compulsive kiss that seemed to drag her soul out of her body. She went limp beneath him as sensation drowned thought, their bare chests glued together, the contact of skin with skin sending shivers of ecstasy along her nerves. Then suddenly he rolled away from her and lay on his back, a hand shielding his eyes.

'You're like heady wine,' he murmured thickly, 'witches' brew.'

Sancia raised herself on her elbow and stared at him while the tumult in her blood slowly subsided. Rick, satisfied that he had asserted his mastery over her, seemed to have fallen asleep. She knew she had been within an inch of surrendering to him completely, shamelessly in a semi-public place, for although no one

was in sight they could have been interrupted at any
moment. Once he had asked her if she could resist him
and she had replied that she couldn't if he loved her, but
he didn't love her, she was not so naïve that she did not
know he had only felt desire. He had told her not to
confuse love with sex, and she *could not* be in love with
such a recent acquaintance. Sex, that was all this turmoil
in her senses whenever he touched her must be. But it *was*
more than mere physical response, since only in his
presence did she come fully alive. Like the statue in the
legend that had been animated at the wish of her creator,
who loved her, Rick had in a sense recreated her,
awakened her dormant sexuality. It had started with the
witches' brew to which he had referred, and it seemed
she had fallen under a spell that was not altogether
benign.

Rick's breathing had quietened as whatever had
excited him abated. His long, black lashes covered his
eyes, lashes any girl would have envied, shadowing his
olive cheeks. Sancia turned her head away, aware that
she wanted to touch them, and dug her fingers into the
sand, letting it sift through her fingers while she tried to
sort out her confused thoughts.

She knew from her grandmother's hints that she
wanted a match between herself and Gio, who had
turned out to be Rick. Was it also his wish, and was he
going to propose to her? He had told her that in his
boyhood Lucia had seemed to him to be the loveliest
thing he had ever seen, and she knew she resembled her
mother. But though he might appreciate her looks, she
was still hopelessly unsophisticated and he was a man of
wide experience, who probably found her childish. If he
did propose it would be to please Nonna and acquire the
Casa Antonelli, the long cherished plan that Lucia had

thwarted. Could she ever hope to win from him a deeper and more lasting emotion than a passing fancy? It seemed unlikely. She glanced at his recumbent figure and sighed. Was physical attraction a stable foundation for marriage? Him being the nationality he was, she had little hope of his fidelity. Could she be a complacent wife?

Well, he hadn't proposed yet; probably he never would and she would not have to make such a momentous decision. There must be other women in his life with possibly a stronger claim. She sighed again, envisaging sultry Latin beauties who could give him greater satisfaction than she ever could. Perhaps she would be wise to resist her grandmother's pleadings and return to England with Judy when their holiday was ended. Somehow the prospect was bleak. Rick embodied all the colour and warmth that she had missed in her austere life. She put out a tentative hand, moved by an almost irresistible desire to touch him, and hastily drew it back. She didn't want to invite another violent demonstration, not until she was more certain ... certain of what? Her feelings or his? He was still in many ways a stranger to her, but that was part of his fascination. Boys like Tim were too obvious; Rick was an enigma. He was more than eligible from a worldly point of view, but she was not mercenary, and though it seemed she was able to turn him on, any good-looking woman could do that. It was unfair that only he could have the same effect upon herself.

She saw Judy and Enrico coming towards them from wherever they had hidden themselves. Enrico looked sulky, and when he sought to take Judy's hand, she petulantly snatched it away. Sancia surmised that he no longer satisfied Judy now she had scented more exciting prey, and recalled with something like dismay that she had told her friend she was not interested in Rick, and she could go ahead. But that wasn't a bad thing, for if Rick succumbed to Judy's wiles, it would show the shallowness of his protestations, and that he had no serious intentions towards herself.

Judy hastened her steps when she saw them and dropped down on her knees beside Rick.

'Wake up, Sleeping Beauty, I'm hungry.'

Rick opened his eyes and gave her a languid smile. 'You should wake me with a kiss.'

Sancia turned her head away as a laughing Judy bent over him, a black arrow of jealousy piercing her. Whether Judy did actually kiss Rick, she did not see, but she caught Enrico's savage look as she scrambled to her feet.

'Where are we going to eat?' she asked brightly, though she felt no desire for food.

'The Regina, of course.' Rick pushed Judy over on to the sand and sprang to his feet in one swift agile movement, his body was perfectly co-ordinated. 'Enrico, keep your woman in order, and Sancia, go and get dressed.'

'I'm not Enrico's woman, I'm free for all,' Judy declared, picking herself up and giving Rick a languishing look.

'How nice,' he returned drily, and strode away towards the bathing huts. He did not fancy Judy! Sancia felt suddenly elated.

Lunch was a lively meal, all tensions forgotten and the two men vying with each other to entertain the girls. Sancia and Judy had made sketchy toilets in the wooden cabins on the beach provided for changing. Judy's scarlet pyjamas were split to the knee on either side and

combined with the scantiest of tops. She had managed an
elaborate make-up, and with her bush of black hair
presented an exotic appearance. Sancia hadn't bothered
with make-up beyond a touch of lip salve and a dash of
powder. Kind nature had given her long dark eyelashes
that didn't need mascara, fringing her green eyes and
contrasting with her vivid red-gold hair. A new
animation brought a glow to her cheeks and a shine to
her eyes; she looked quite lovely, and Rick was giving
her those keen, assessing glances he had so often
bestowed upon her before, as if deciding whether she
were worth the sacrifice of his freedom—plus the
palazzo, of course. The thought brought a defiant sparkle
into Sancia's eyes, and she demanded:

'What are you hoping to find, Rick? You look at me as
if you were trying to dissect me!'

'Perhaps I want to discover what makes you tick.'

'My heart, of course,' she retorted, 'as theirs does
everyone else.'

'And the heart has its secrets?'

'Naturally, but they're not for publication.'

'Then be careful, your eyes and mouth may betray
them.' He smiled mockingly. 'They are traitorous organs,
mia cara.'

She caught her breath—was she showing too plainly
how he stimulated her? Twirling her wine glass—they
had been drinking red wine—she declared, 'They don't
express truth, only the emotions engendered by alcohol.
No, no more,' she put her hand over her glass as Rick
made to refill it, 'it might be as potent as Paula's witches'
brew.'

She eyed him closely to see if he reacted to Paula's
name, but there was no change in his expression.

'Poor Paula, I'm afraid the spell didn't work for her,' she murmured.

'She hadn't got a *palazzo* up her sleeve,' Judy interposed spitefully. She was chagrined that Rick was giving Sancia all his attention.

That damned *palazzo*, Sancia thought bitterly, which had been poor Lucia's bane and seemed likely to be hers also, for whatever he might do or say, she would always suspect that the desire for its ownership was what was motivating him. Why didn't her grandmother leave it to him when he was so obviously the best person to have it? The Rossinis were all dead. But so far nothing definite had been said, only hints and surmises, and she would reserve her forces until it was, for, she resolved, glancing at Rick at little wistfully, she would not be cajoled into a loveless marriage, however much he attracted her.

Though he had called her chicken, Rick yielded to Judy's plea not to go so fast on their homeward journey, which consideration Sancia marked up in his favour. Venice rose up from the waters as they cruised over the lagoon towards it, its domes and palaces lit by the sun. Sancia recalled that her father had said even a dog would feel romantic in that fairy city, but the hard-bitten Rick would be impervious to its magic.

CHAPTER SIX

RICK left for Milan early the next morning upon receipt of an urgent telephone call the night before, a reminder that he was first and foremost an efficient and conscientious business executive. He promised to return before the girls' holiday ended and would perhaps take them up into the mountains. He kept his car parked on the mainland where it was easily available.

Sancia felt deflated. He was taking it for granted that she would be returning with Judy, and all her conjectures and apprehensions had been quite unnecessary. Nor apparently had Nonna told him that she wanted Sancia to stay with her, which implied that such an arrangement was of no interest to him. As for matrimony, that was very far from his thoughts. At dinner all his attention had been focused on the Contessa, then the call had come, and he had excused himself on the plea of papers to study.

'Such devotion to duty,' Nonna had remarked when he had left the *salotto*, but she looked disappointed. She didn't ask Sancia to come to her room that night. Sancia felt that in some way she had failed, but she could not think how. Judy was out with Enrico, and she spent the evening on her balcony watching the waters of the Grand Canal glide by, feeling extremely flat.

She had been so certain, when her grandmother talked about a rich husband, that she had had Rick in mind, but either she had been mistaken, or else Rick had told the old lady that such a union was unpalatable, which would

94

account for her disappointed look. Upon reflection it became obvious that with all his interests being in Milan, a Venetian palace would only be a burden to him. The Contessa was very old, and had lost touch with reality. Sancia had been a fool to take any of her utterances seriously.

They continued with their normal routine for the next week, and Sancia went eagerly to the Contessa's room, hoping she would talk about Rick. He was beginning to obsess her, and she longed for further information which might throw light upon his elusive personality. But the old lady barely mentioned him; all her talk was about arrangements for Sancia to come and live with her, about which she was still determined.

'Does Rick approve of it?' Sancia asked boldly.

'I wish you would not use that silly name,' the Contessa said peevishly. 'Call him Riccardo, or if you prefer an abbreviation, Gio, like I do. "Rick" is not Italian.'

'Does Signor Antonelli approve of my coming to live with you?' Sancia reformed her question.

'Naturally he does. He has advocated that I should obtain a companion ever since poor Lucia died.'

Which to Sancia was a very unsatisfactory reply. Apparently Rick had not objected, but she did not want to live at the *palazzo* to provide him with amorous diversion on his flying visits, which seemed to be all he wanted from her. She could hardly tell her grandmother that. She wondered how the Contessa expected her to find an affluent husband if she never met anybody suitable. She became convinced that the old lady suffered from delusions. But she didn't want to leave her, for she was the only person who needed her, although the promised introduction to English pupils did not seem to be forthcoming. Perhaps Rick would suggest that she was paid a salary for the care of her grandmother, but that idea she found distasteful. She suspected it would be his money, and she didn't want to be beholden to him.

She was still in a state of indecision when, at the beginning of their last week of vacation, Rick came again. This time it was at night. Sancia was sitting on the Contessa's bed, wearing a black kaftan with gold embroidery, which was loose and cool, for the days were becoming very hot. Her hair hung, a red-gold mass, about her shoulders. They heard quick footsteps crossing the *salotto*, and he erupted into the room, his arms full of roses. Sancia sprang to her feet, as he dropped the mass of blooms on to the bed.

'With all my love, Nonna.' He detached a small bunch of white ones. 'These are for you, Sancia.' And he held them out to her.

She took them automatically, aware that she had coloured and that her pulses were racing. He was all in black—a sweater and cords, for the voyage across the lagoon would have been chilly in spite of the warm weather. She was reminded vividly of the first time she had seen him, and involuntarily her eyes went to his broad chest, half expecting to see Yorick's skull.

'Naughty boy!' The Contessa's wrinkled face had lit up as it always did when she saw Rick. 'Bursting into a lady's bedroom without a by-your-leave.' She chuckled. 'But I don't suppose it holds any secrets for you.'

'And you're a wicked old girl,' Rick returned, kissing her. He surveyed her a little anxiously. '*Come sta, carissima?*'

She replied in Italian, and thinking they would like to be alone, Sancia moved towards the door.

'Don't go, Sancia.' His imperious command halted her. 'Nonna, I will see you in the morning, but now it's time you slept. I want to have a word with Sancia in the *salotto*.'

A meaningful look passed between them, and Sancia's heart missed a beat. She was reluctant to be alone with Rick.

'I must put my flowers in water,' she said quickly, looking at the pure white blooms she held. Were they meant to be symbolical?

'Bianca will see to them,' Rick returned, taking them from her and putting them with the others. 'Nonna, you permit?'

'*Si, si,*' the old woman said eagerly. 'Bianca will attend to me.'

There were two doors to the bedroom, one opening on to a passage, the other leading into the *salotto*. Rick indicated the latter and waited for her to precede him. It was still ajar after his precipitous entrance. Sancia hesitated; there was an air of purposefulness about him that she distrusted.

'Can't it wait until the morning?' she asked nervously.

His eyes were glittering as they had through his mask on Walpurgis Night and he looked a little menacing.

'No, it can't,' he snapped. 'I've already procrastinated for too long.'

Unwillingly she passed into the other room.

It was full of eerie light—the servants had not yet drawn the shutters, though they had cleared the big polished table that they used for meals, the vast apartment serving both as dining and sitting room. The water outside was reflected in the mirrors, and the unlit chandeliers above them shimmered with ghostly radiance. Sancia moved across to the window, painfully conscious of Rick close behind her. When she reached it, she pushed one section open and stepped out on to the balcony. Above her was the starry night, below, the water reflecting the lighted windows of the other palaces. Somewhere below a youth was singing to the notes of a guitar, but not, alas, a serenade, only some popular favourite.

Rick's arms closed round her from behind, holding her against his chest.

'Where are you going, *mia cara*, into the canal?' His mouth was against her ear. 'You can't escape me, you know.'

'Rick, please, no more of that,' she begged as her blood began to take fire. 'I'm not . . .'

'Not what? An icicle?' He was laughing at her. 'Too true, you've melted now.' His hand was pressed over her throbbing heart.

She tried to free herself. 'Rick, I'm not like . . . my mother.'

'No, *grazie a Dio*.'

He released her so suddenly that she had to clutch at the balustrade for support.

'Come inside,' he bade her in quite a different tone, and as she followed him, 'and let's have a little illumination; this twilight may be very romantic, but I want to see your face.'

The room was flooded with amber radiance as he switched on the chandeliers, their glass pendants tinkling faintly in the draught from the window. They shone on Sancia's slender figure in black and gold, the glory of her hair and her pale face with wide pleading eyes.

'*Dio mio*, but you're beautiful!' Rick exclaimed. 'But don't look so scared. What do you imagine I'm going to do to you?'

'It's what you've done already,' she said sadly. 'You

haven't much mercy, have you?'

He looked startled, raising a slanted eyebrow.

'What on earth do you mean?'

'That I was happier when I was frozen.'

'Nonsense. I brought you to life. You can't want to exist as a lovely robot, all your potential wasted.'

She smiled wanly. 'Robots don't have any feelings.'

He looked at her intently. 'And you're finding yours too strong for you?'

'Uncomfortably so,' she admitted frankly. 'Rick, I'll be no man's mistress.' She raised her head proudly, and prayed she would have the strength to keep her resolve.

'What the devil are you talking about, who wants you to be his mistress?' he demanded. 'Oh, I get it.' A slow smile dawned in his eyes. 'As if I'd so dishonour you, but then you're familiar with a permissive society.' He drew his heels together and made her one of his mocking bows. 'Sancia Everard, I, Giovanni Riccardo Antonelli, am asking you to be my wife.'

'Oh,' she murmured faintly.

He drew his slanted brows together, giving him a demonic look.

'Is that all you have to say? Oh? You can't be surprised, Nonna has been hinting at a marriage between us ever since you arrived. In fact I believe she mentioned it to your father when she wrote, and he thought it was an excellent idea.'

So that was why Dr Everard hadn't let her see the Contessa's letter. Sancia sank down on one of the armchairs, feeling her legs would no longer support her.

'They all know you want the *palazzo*,' she said dully. For that was why he had proposed, and to learn that her father had been willing to hand her over to a man he hadn't even met simply to get her out of his hair was an added smart. Thinking more of his callousness than Rick's motives, which she had already suspected, she went on bitterly, 'I suppose if I'd been as fat as a hippopotamus and as spiteful as an adder, you'd still have taken me. It must have been an enormous relief when you inspected me in London to discover I wasn't exactly repulsive.'

Rick's eyes flashed grey fire and he seemed on the verge of a violent outburst. He strode across the room and shut the window with a bang. But when he turned about he was urbane and smiling.

'In this country it is usual for the bride to have a dowry, and only recently have women of good family married for love. It is still regarded as a business arrangement. The *casa* will be your portion, and my money will renovate it.'

She held up her hand. 'Oh, please, I've heard all that. It's why your grandfather married Nonna.'

'And it worked. They became devoted to each other.'

'You mean she did to him, conveniently.' She was recalling Giovanni Antonelli's arrogant features, his despotic attitude towards poor Lucia. 'I'd be surprised if your grandfather loved anyone in his whole life.'

'How can you judge? He was dead long before you came here.'

'I've seen his photograph, it was very revealing.'

'You have got your knife into him, but what's he got to do with us?'

She couldn't say she feared he was another of the same sort. To love him and be treated with casual indifference would be hell.

'There's more to marriage than dowries and suitability,' she said hesitantly.

He grinned wickedly. 'Considerably more, but we

seem to be sexually compatible, so I don't think you need worry about that.'

She blushed fierily, turning her head away. So he had had the audacity to make sure of that before he made his offer.

He laughed at her embarrassment and told her, 'I thought you modern girls went in for plain speaking, but let us be serious. It's time I married, and I don't suppose you want to return to that sanctimonious father of yours?'

'Oh no,' she cried, wincing, knowing how unwelcome she would be. She twisted her hands together, wondering if she dare mention love, but probably he would think she was a sentimental little fool to expect more than the physical gratification he could give her.

Rick frowned down upon her bent, bright head. 'Well, then?'

'I don't know. Oh, I don't know.'

'Then perhaps this will make up your mind for you.'

He swooped. All his restrained anger was released in his almost savage kisses, the hands that mercilessly explored her body. Through the disintegration of her senses, Sancia clung to one thought. He doesn't love me, this isn't love. Can I marry him without love? For love, to her way of thinking, sanctified and justified the physical act; without it, it was degrading. When, spent and exhausted, she lay back in his arms and saw the triumph gleaming in his eyes, she made a desperate appeal:

'If only you loved me!'

'Oh, bah!' he ejaculated, and kissed her again. 'Isn't this enough?'

Her senses clamoured, it is, it is, but she knew it wasn't.

He, however, seemed satisfied that he had overcome her resistance, for later, when both were calmer, he declared, 'Tomorrow we'll announce our engagement.'

'Oh, please not yet,' she pleaded, 'not yet. I must have a little time to . . . to adjust myself.'

'*Dio mio*, what for?' Rick spoke almost roughly. 'I want to get this thing settled, Sancia. You will continue to live here until we are married; I believe you've already considered that?' She nodded. 'It may not be for very long. Nonna is very frail, she has a heart condition.'

Sancia had not known that, but it accounted for Rick's solicitude and the many hours of rest the old woman needed.

'I . . . I'm sorry to hear that.'

'I thought I'd better put you wise. With care she may survive several years longer.' He sighed. Always this tender concern for the woman who had fostered him, would he ever feel it for Sancia?

'I won't ever leave her,' she promised.

He looked relieved. 'That would be best. I can commute between here and Milano. There is an air service. Renovations ought to be started at once; I think we can do them without disturbing her.' He sprang to his feet and began to pace the marble floor. 'It will be a big job, an interesting job. We want to retain all its beauty while making it secure. The damp is the worst problem. Venice is sinking, you know that? But I think we can preserve it for many years to come.' He went to the window and ran his finger down the frame. 'This is rotting—I was afraid so. All this will have to be replaced.'

Sancia watched him sadly; already she was out of his mind as he planned what could be done to the possession she would bring him. This was no lovers' talk. Were stones and mortar so much more important to him than her thoughts and emotions? She understood his obsession with the beautiful old building up to a point. She was beginning to love it herself, and it would be a bond between them, as was their joint affection for the old woman in the next room. Her body was bruised by his violent love-play, her mouth felt swollen, they had shared a mutual passion, but hadn't it been partly simulated on his part, to bend her to his will? As for herself, he would rapidly become her whole existence; already he dominated her, quelling her feeble resistance with his mastery. Was she, who had always stood up for feminine independence, who had championed Lucia when they condemned her, about to become a doormat? Could she possibly be happy in a subservient position? Yet Rick had only to take her in his arms again and she would become as weak as a newborn kitten. Nor could she face the prospect of a life without him.

She sighed, and rose to her feet.

'I'll say goodnight, Rick. I've a lot to think about.'

He came across to her, putting his hands on her shoulders.

'Don't think too much, *mia bella*, let yourself feel.'

He kissed her absently, his mind still full of the *palazzo*. 'I shall be here for a few days, Sancia, and I'll make arrangements for an immediate wedding.'

She quailed. 'So soon?'

'What is there to wait for?' He looked at her searchingly and her eyes dropped before his intent gaze. 'You're not afraid of me, are you, Sancia?'

She was—a little. Never could she quite shake off her first impression of him, a dark menacing figure; besides, he was so dynamic, so sure of himself, while she was full of hesitations. She had met him masked, with a skull hanging from his neck, and he was still in a sense disguised, she knew so little of the real man beneath his outward seeming.

'No,' she told him, 'and after all, marriage nowadays is not irrevocable.'

His hands on her shoulders tightened to a grip. 'That's not a nice thing to say! Make no mistake, Sancia, ours will be; I don't believe in divorce. What I have I hold.'

He released her shoulders and flicked her lightly under the chin. '*Mia cara*, you look as though you expected me to beat you. I promise you I'll never do that.' Again he was laughing at her, his eyes alight with merriment. He did not take her reluctance seriously, well knowing he could overcome it with an embrace. 'Go to bed now and dream of me,' he commanded. 'You look tired. If Nonna isn't asleep, I'll tell her all is settled as she has long planned.'

He kissed her again, with a little more fervour, and Sancia slowly made her way upstairs. His last words had chilled her. It had been planned, another union between Antonelli and Rossini, to keep the *palazzo* in the family, before she had been consulted. Even her father's consent and approval had been obtained. They had been sure Rick's charisma would cause her to fall for him, and she would present no problem. How she wished the house was not an issue, that Rick wanted to marry her because she was the one woman above all others he desired, but she felt sure that without her dowry, he wouldn't have given her a second thought.

'You should be on top of the world,' Judy exclaimed, when Sancia had told her she would not be returning to London with her and why. 'So you've changed your mind about him. I thought that was happening. I'm not dim, and I soon realised he was quite impervious to my wiles. Congratulations, he's got everything. But why the dismal look, aren't you elated?'

'He doesn't love me,' Sancia said forlornly.

'Of course he does, why else should he ask you to marry him?'

'Haven't you yet grasped that this wretched house is all they think about? The Contessa considers it's my heritage, and she wants us to wed so Rick can share it. He's crazy to renovate it, and is marrying me to get possession of it.'

'Well, that's a nice harmless hobby, much better than the things some men get up to. But why are you so sure he doesn't love you?'

'He . . . he's never said so.'

'Perhaps he's shy?' suggested Judy.

Sancia had to laugh. 'Rick, shy!'

'Some men are, you know, when it comes to expressing their deepest feelings, and I must say I sicken of the way that poor little word is bandied about when what is really meant is bed. Love means unselfishness, consideration, denial of self.' Sancia stared at Judy in astonishment, never having heard her express such sentiments before. 'If it were practised more there'd be less divorce. But you surprise me; being Italian, I should have thought our Ricky would be lavish with flowery phrases, even if he didn't mean them.'

'Thank God he isn't,' Sancia cried vehemently. 'I'd hate him to be insincere.'

'You can't have it all ways,' Judy said sagely. 'But you haven't anything to worry about. He's rich, handsome and passionate, so what if it is this mouldy palace he's after? It could do with a lick of paint anyway. Give him a couple of babies and he'll adore you. Italians think such a lot of family.'

Sancia flushed and paled at the picture Judy had

conjured up. Naturally Rick would want children, probably a large family. That important subject had not been mentioned between them, but it had all happened so suddenly. She saw herself installed at the *casa* with a brood of young Antonellis, while Rick . . . what would he be doing during her numerous confinements? Amusing himself in Milan between weekends in Venice? Business entertainment could cover a multitude of sins. Was that what she wanted? She was only twenty, and she would like a little life before she was swamped in domesticity. Only a deep reciprocal love could make such an existence a happy one, when the volcanic fire of passion had subsided into routine. She wasn't quite sure that her feelings for him were lasting ones. She had been swept off her feet, and when she came back to earth she might find that she had made as ghastly a mistake as her mother had done before her. She needed time to think the matter through, to examaine her own emotions, to be sure, but time was to be denied her.

Rick took them on the promised expedition to Lake Garda, a long day trip including a cruise on the lake in a steamer. He did not suggest Enrico should accompany them this time, and to Sancia's pique he paid more attention to Judy than to herself. Judy could be very amusing when she wished, and Sancia found herself unable to join in their lively banter. Rick was arranging for their wedding three weeks hence, a civil ceremony as they belonged to different denominations, but completely binding, he assured her. Religion was another subject they had not touched upon, and it seemed to her with so many serious matters for discussion, frivolous badinage was out of place, but Rick seemed anxious to avoid being alone with her. There had been no more physical demonstrations. She returned from Garda dispirited and uneasy.

'Really, Sancia, you should try to be a little more vivacious,' Judy chided her as they went up to dress that evening. 'You acted as if you were jealous of poor well-meaning me. That's not the way to make him love you, if you persist in believing he doesn't.'

'Perhaps I was a little jealous,' Sancia admitted. 'You both seemed so light-hearted, and somehow I couldn't join in. I've too much on my mind just now.'

Judy looked at her with affectionate contempt. 'Why don't you leave everything to him and enjoy yourself? But you always were a nit where men were concerned. I don't believe much in romantic love myself, but if that's what you want, I'm sure you could get it if you went the right way about it.'

Ah, if only she could.

Desperate for reassurance, Sancia waylaid Rick the next afternoon when he returned from a trip across to the mainland to get his car serviced. In the house, either the Contessa or Judy was present. Crowded *vaporetti* and black gondolas passed up and down as she stood waiting beneath the stone archway that gave admittance to the landing stage. Before her were the stout mooring poles painted with the striped Rossini colours, red and white. She had learned that the poles carried the tints of their owners'—or past owners'—escutcheons, though many had been overlaid with the patina of age. She, the last descendant of the once proud Rossinis, looked at them curiously. Together with the coat of arms above the archway, they belonged to a distant age of pomp and circumstance when armorial bearings had been signifi-cant. They were meaningless now.

The speedboat came in with a swirl of spray and Rick

sprang ashore, carrying the painter.

As always, the sudden sight of him set her pulses galloping. In the strong sunlight his hair had the sheen of a rook's wings, and tanned arms and legs were exposed to its rays, for he wore only shorts and a sleeveless singlet.

'Sancia, what are you doing here?' he exclaimed, as he secured the boat to its moorings, and she, fascinated, watched the muscles rippling in his back under the thin material as he did so.

'I'm waiting for you.'

He came to stand beside her, grey eyes questioning.

'Is anything wrong?'

'No . . . yes.' She raised anxious green eyes to him. 'Rick, why have you become so aloof?'

'Am I?'

She fidgeted with the belt of her dress, and drooped her head. 'I've been wondering if perhaps you're having second thoughts about our . . . our marriage.'

As she said the words it flashed into her mind that if he cried off her world would become a desert, so utterly had he come to fill her whole horizon.

Rick made a movement towards her, then thrust his hands into his trouser pockets and turned to look at the water.

'You needn't wonder, I've no intention of letting you go.'

'Of course, you'd lose the *palazzo*,' she said bitterly.

'Damn the *palazzo*!' He swung round to look at her, and his eyes were smouldering. '*Mia cara*, there are flames which if ignited cannot be extinguished, and you are a match to my tinder. *Patienza*, we have not long to wait.'

It wasn't quite what she wanted to hear, and she blushed vividly as she veiled her eyes from that burning gaze. Not long before she became his, body and soul, though perhaps souls hadn't much to do with it.

Greatly daring, she asked timidly, 'Then you do ... love me a little, it isn't only the *palazzo*?'

He gave her a brooding look. 'The *palazzo* is only incidental.' Then his face changed, broke into a charming smile, and the sultry atmosphere between them was dispelled.

'*Mia cara*, I adore you,' he said lightly, too lightly. 'But don't let's stay here broiling in the sun. Shall we join Nonna?'

Sancia preceded him up the worn stone steps, dissatisfied. Always he avoided saying the three words she longed to hear. Perhaps he was too honest to perjure himself, nor did she believe the *casa* was not of prime importance to him.

'Have you ever been really in love?' she persisted as they reached the shaded *salotto*.

'Oh, many times,' he returned. 'I'm not a monk, you know—but don't try to delve into my past, Sancia, that's all over. I intend to be a model husband.'

The Contessa waved to them from her armchair, and as they went towards her, Sancia reflected that the road to hell was supposed to be paved with good intentions; she wondered if Rick had become too cynical to be capable of really loving any woman.

CHAPTER SEVEN

JUDY went back to England and Rick returned to Milan. Sancia wrote to her father to tell him her news. Except for sending a few postcards, they had not communicated since she had come to Venice.

Mid-week he rang her up.

'A very satisfactory match,' he told her complacently. 'Antonelli is a man of considerable substance and the house is your joint heritage. I feared when the Contessa first suggested it that he would find you too young and naïve.' (Sancia writhed inwardly.) 'Congratulations upon having pulled it off.'

He then told her that he and Barbara had been married at a register office, and it hadn't seemed worth while breaking into her holiday by asking her to attend it. It had been a very simple affair, only themselves and two witnesses, he hadn't wanted any fuss.

Typical of her egotistical father, Sancia thought, never considering that Barbara would have liked a proper wedding as most girls would.

'Will you be able to come to mine?' she asked. 'It would be a honeymoon trip for Barbara.'

'No, I couldn't get away, I've no time for such frivolities as honeymoons. Besides, I don't think my ex-mother-in-law would welcome my presence or Barbara's.' Which was true: Nonna had never forgiven him for his treatment of Lucia, and Sancia realised she had been tactless to suggest it. She would have no one of her own to attend her nuptials, for Judy had said she

110

couldn't get away again so soon.

'Well, I hope you'll be happy,' Dr Everard said perfunctorily, and rang off.

Her father had jumped at the idea when it had been put to him in the Contessa's first epistle, as a way of getting his unwanted daughter settled, his only anxiety being that Rick might not accept her. If ever there was an arranged marriage, it's mine, Sancia thought ruefully, and I declared I'd never agree to one. Everyone had conspired to bring it about, and for all the wrong reasons. She felt like a pawn in a game of chess that had been sacrificed to the black knight to bring about a successful conclusion. Would her grandmother have become alienated if she had refused to marry Rick? She had become attached to the old lady, and the thought was painful, but she did not believe the Contessa would have thrown her out; more probably she would have had to endure endless reproaches, in the hope that she would change her mind. Come to think of it, she had not actually given her consent. Rick had rushed her into an engagement, taking it for granted after he had kissed her into submission. In her saner moments it would seem she had been quite crazy, but Judy insisted she was fortunate to have captured such a prize, and when she was in Rick's presence, all thought of rebellion faded. She was lucky and she couldn't expect not to find a few snarls, the greatest being the dread that he would neglect her once he had obtained the object of his dreams—which was not herself.

Sancia had acquired a new companion. She had found Beppo in the back yard. He had crept through a hole in the wall—another thing needing repair—with a brick tied round his neck, having been thrown into the canal to drown. But he had managed to struggle out and sought the nearest hiding place. He was starving, his bones sticking through his bedraggled coat, and he hadn't tried to bite her while she detached the brick, but looked up at her with piteous beseeching eyes. He was a mongrel of mixed breed, more like a small collie than anything else, and, washed and fed, he looked quite a handsome dog. The servants muttered about rabies and fleas, but Sancia was determined to keep him. Rick raised no objection, beyond saying that if she must have a dog he would have preferred one with a pedigree. Sancia retorted that she didn't think a lot of pedigrees, and the stray had been sent to her by providence. He would be a protection for her when she took an evening stroll. That had diverted him. She must never go out alone after dusk; that was an order. Sancia looked meek and said nothing, she didn't intend to obey him.

Rick came for the last weekend before she was to become his wife. Meanwhile the Contessa had insisted upon buying her a 'trousseau', as she termed it. (Shades of Victoriana!) To please her, Sancia went shopping with Bianca at the best Venetian shops. They bought piles of diaphanous underwear, silk dresses and knitwear, to be put down to the Contessa's account. She lost track of the thousands of lire expended, for she was always confused by the number of noughts in the Italian currency; ten thousand lire was actually under five pounds. Her grandmother insisted she must be kitted out as befitted a member of the Italian aristocracy, though most of the remainder of that seemed to be poverty-stricken. Rick had bought her a ring, a semi-circle of small emeralds 'to match your eyes'. None of it felt quite real. She seemed to be existing in a dream world, a fairy tale that would end at midnight, and she would wake up and find herself back in her office, and living with Judy.

Rick arrived on the Friday night, coming as usual by boat. Sancia could never meet him without a turbulence in her whole being, eyes sparkling, the quick colour coming and going under her thin skin, her emotion all the greater for a slight tinge of fear. She was about to give herself wholly into the keeping of this dark, enigmatic man who was still almost a stranger to her, that was to say as regarded any real intimacy, and about to cleave to him for the rest of her life. It was an exciting prospect, but also a little daunting.

He greeted her with his usual perfunctory kiss which she found so unsatisfactory—but he had given his reason for his lack of ardour. There was a glint in his eyes as he told her, 'only another week'. But this evening he seemed more than usually preoccupied, so much so, that Nonna asked if anything had gone wrong with his business. He assured her over dinner, which they took together, that everything was fine; Mancellis was prospering in spite of the recession. But when they had finished he begged to be excused. He had to meet an important client, but he would see them in the morning.

'Strange time to do business,' complained the Contessa. She was looking a little flushed, although she insisted she was perfectly well. 'I thought you left that behind in Milano.'

'He's passing through and it's the only time I can catch him,' Rick explained.

He was still wearing his business suit, a beautifully-cut creation in dark grey cloth that made him look very elegant. Sancia thought how handsome and distinguished he looked as he said goodnight.

'He must be tired,' Nonna said, disgruntled by his departure. 'But he always puts duty first. That is how he has got where he is.'

Sancia, with an empty evening in front of her, felt restless and disappointed. She decided she would go for a stroll before her usual bedtime chat with her grandmother. It was a close evening, and she felt stifled in the house. She did not mention her intention, knowing it would meet with a protest and the reminder that Rick had forbidden nocturnal wanderings, but with Beppo to protect her, she couldn't come to harm. As an added precaution, she borrowed a black shawl from Bianca, the kind that peasant women wore, and with it draped over her head and shoulders, over her black dress, she would be completely inconspicuous. Beppo, who was banished to the kitchen regions when Rick was there for dinner, greeted her with joy, and they slipped out of the back way together.

She went through the labyrinth of small streets to the Rialto Bridge, crossed it and went into a further maze of narrow passageways, walking swiftly and oblivious of curious male glances thrown in her direction. '*Una religiosa*,' they decided, and shrugged.

Finally she came to one of the innumerable *campos*, a wide space surrounding a church. This one provided the unusual amenities of a seat and a drinking trough, which permitted the dog to assuage his thirst. Sancia sat down in the shadow of the church, and he lay down behind her feet and went to sleep.

At the other side of the square there was a café where a few customers still lingered at the tables set out in front of it. Watching them idly, Sancia suddenly became tense. One of them, a man in a grey suit, was Rick. He was with a girl who had her back to Sancia; all she could see of her was long black hair streaming over her shoulders. She was wearing the universal shirt and jeans, and seemed to be very agitated from the movements of her gesticulating hands. So that was the client whom Rick had gone off to meet! But could it be Rick? He turned to beckon to a waiter, and the light streaming out from the café interior illuminated his face. There was no mistaking that profile, the arrogant carriage of his dark head. But who was his companion? She was too youthful and too meanly clad to be associated with a business deal.

Sancia shivered and drew her shawl more closely around her in spite of the warm air. Always she had feared to discover some other woman in Rick's life; had she stumbled upon a secret assignation? She didn't look the sort to appeal to him, especially as she was wearing trousers; was she some waif he had befriended? But that was most unlikely, and he had deliberately deceived her and the Contessa, implying he was going to meet a man.

The couple rose from the table, and Rick put his arm about the girl's shoulders as they came towards her. Sancia looked round, wondering where she could hide, but she was in dense shadow, and they were so absorbed in each other they probably wouldn't notice her. She hunched her shoulders as an old woman would, and Beppo never stirred. They halted within earshot and the girl flung her arms about Rick's neck. Evidently she had been crying, and her slight figure was shaking with emotion.

'Caro ... carissimo ...' she sobbed, then to Sancia's surprise went on in English. 'You say not, but I know when you are married, you will forget me.'

'I swear I won't,' Rick declared emphatically. 'Mia bambina, amore mia, it will make no difference. Everything will be exactly as it was before. Don't cry, there is nothing to weep about.'

He was stroking her hair back from her face and Sancia had never heard such tenderness in his voice except occasionally when he spoke to Nonna. The girl clung to him and he laid his face against her wet cheek. Whoever she was, he loved her, of that Sancia felt sure.

He said something Sancia could not catch, and gently disengaged her clinging arms. Putting one of his arms around her waist and drawing her against his side, they moved away, the dark head against his shoulder, to disappear down a side street, with never a glance towards the huddled figure on the seat. Sancia sat on, stunned by his duplicity, until Beppo, waking from a dream of chasing rabbits, yawned, stretched and came to lick her hand.

When she was once more in her own room, Sancia rang for Bianca to return the shawl.

'And please ask the Contessa to excuse me tonight. I have a headache.'

'*Si, si, signorina.*' The maid looked commiseratingly at Sancia's white face. She knew all about her nocturnal wanderings and put her own interpretation upon them: Signor Riccardo was so often away and she did not blame his *fidanzata* for seeking diversion on the side; she believed that was why Sancia had asked her not to mention them to the Contessa.

'Somet'ing go wrong, *si*? I getta you hot drink?'

'No, everything's all right and I don't want anything. It's just a headache. I'll take some aspirin and lie down.'

But everything was *not* all right. The recollection of Rick's face as he looked at the girl he loved haunted her. She had had hopes of winning his heart herself, and now she had discovered it was bestowed elsewhere, and that he had declared his marriage 'would make no difference'. It had occurred to her more than once that Rick might have an attachment in Milan, but that city was a long way away, and he had told her she must visit it soon and see where he lodged and worked, which did not sound as if he had anything to hide. And he had said his past was behind him. If he had had a mistress, she imagined she would have been a stylish, experienced woman of the world, who would have accepted their parting with a resigned shrug. But the girl in the *campo* had been no older than herself and she certainly wasn't smart. She spoke English and in an educated voice, some drop-out from a cultured family perhaps, there were many of them roaming Europe in search of adventure. Their liaison appeared to have been of some duration, and probably he had installed her in a love nest in one of the back streets of Venice. With a surge of despairing jealousy, Sancia visualised them at that moment, lying in each other's arms, shrouded in that long black hair. He must be in the habit of visiting her during his weekends in Venice; when he slept at the *palazzo* he occupied a bedroom at the back of it, next to the Contessa's. Outside it were the remnants of what had once been a stairway up from the yard—another thing to be repaired—and it would be easy for an agile man to climb down and be away without anyone being any the wiser, to return before dawn. So romantic, oh, so very romantic, while he was wooing her unsuspecting self.

Although he loved the girl, he would never consider marrying her. She did not have a *palazzo* for her dowry, probably nothing to offer except her heart. Sancia felt pity for her, but perhaps she didn't need it, being one of those who opted for 'free' love, and as Rick had assured her the present arrangement would continue, she was content. The Contessa would make light of the situation if she confided in her; boys, she would say, will be boys, and such affairs had nothing to do with the serious business of marriage. Only girls must not be girls, Sancia thought savagely, thinking of her mother. The Contessa herself had married Giovanni Antonelli out of expediency, which union, Rick had told her cynically, had been a success. His wife became devoted to him, but had Giovanni been devoted to her? Many Italians kept mistresses and their wives looked the other way, though Rick with his tongue in his cheek had told her he meant to be a model husband, and tonight had lied, saying he was going to meet a client.

Sancia felt suddenly sick, revolting from the whole business. She was being rushed into marriage with a man who had no love for her to secure a heritage which might evade him if the frail old woman died before he acquired it. For that was the stark, bitter truth. He no doubt thought the material advantages she would gain were sufficient compensation for his infidelity, and to a lot of girls that might be so, but not to her. She never had yearned for wealth and a soft life; she wanted love and affection, which seemed to be for ever denied her. Even her grandmother's fondness was suspect, for she too had set her heart upon this marriage and might turn against her if she broke off her engagement.

Which was what Sancia decided she would do.

Thinking back, she remembered how she had often felt that Rick was never wholly involved with her; she knew now that his lovemaking had been play-acting. He had set out to capture her with a purpose and it had amused him to break down her reserve, awaken her womanhood; in short, melt the icicle, as he put it. He knew he was irresistible and had pursued her with the ardour of a huntsman chasing shy game, but once she was his, legally and physically, what then? Must she share him with another woman? She would be installed like a show piece in his renovated *palazzo* to be exhibited when he brought his friends to be entertained, while his real love awaited him in a back street to whom he would sneak away whenever he found an opportunity.

Never that!

She could not conceive of giving herself to any other man except Rick, but men were different, and Rick would want heirs to his precious palace. He would take her as a duty, and when she lay in his arms, would he try to pretend she was that other woman?

Hatred and jealousy welled up in her, all the fiercer for being the reverse of love. She would not submit to him, she would go back to London, live with Judy and slowly freeze up again into what she had been before she knew Rick. She no longer feared him—he was a liar, a mercenary cheat—and she would throw his ring back in his face.

Anger outweighed heartbreak, and on that resolve, unexpectedly Sancia fell asleep.

Next morning she dressed herself with care in a simple green linen dress, with short sleeves and a demure neckline, her hair secured by a green ribbon in her nape. She used more make-up than usual to disguise her pallor. Green sandals completed her outfit, and her smooth tanned legs were bare. She took off her ring and, carrying it in her hand, went down to confront Rick.

As she had expected, the Contessa was not yet up, and Rick was standing on the balcony outside the *salotto* window, casually dressed in white linen slacks and a silk shirt. He had a sleek look about him—Sancia thought she could account for that—his olive face smoothly shaved, his hair a shining black cap.

He came swiftly into the room to greet her, but stopped short at sight of her stony face, her cold 'Good morning', his brows raised.

'You look like Monte Bianco, *mia cara*. Is anything wrong?'

'There always has been,' she said bitterly, 'only I didn't know it. I've decided I can't marry you, Rick, and I want you to take back your ring.'

She laid the semi-circle of emeralds on the table, and it lay sparkling there, reflecting the light.

He was so still that she glanced at him nervously, but his face was without expression, as he asked quietly:

'Might one ask why you've changed your mind?'

Her glance fell beneath his icy stare, and she began to draw aimlessly with her forefinger on the polished table.

'You were in such a hurry, Rick, you didn't give me time to reflect, but now I realise we're not compatible, and I . . . I don't really want to become Italian. We look at life from completely different angles.'

'You've left it a little late to make such a momentous discovery. Our wedding is fixed for next weekend.'

She quailed before the sarcasm in his voice. She didn't want to tell him her real reason, he would think she had been spying on him, but she might have to do so.

'It's better to discover one is making a mistake before it's too late,' she said steadily. 'And to marry you would be a dreadful one.'

'Suppose you stop spewing out platitudes and tell me what has upset you.' He spoke almost kindly. 'Something has, hasn't it?'

She drew a deep breath. 'I saw you in the *campo* . . . I forget which one it was, last night with . . . your client.'

A flicker of anger . . . or was it guilt? . . . in the intent grey eyes.

'And what the hell were you doing wandering about last night? You know I've forbidden it. Were you alone?'

'Yes, of course.'

'Then don't do it again. It's not safe.'

'Never mind about that,' she said wearily. 'I had Beppo with me, and I was tired of being cooped up here. Who was she?'

He looked suddenly wary. 'That's none of your business.'

'Judging by the way you were behaving I think it is. I don't like lies and deceit, Rick, and I couldn't marry a man I don't trust. It was obvious she . . . meant a lot to you.'

He told her succinctly, 'She does.'

Sancia felt a dart of pain. 'Well, that's it, isn't it?'

'Nothing of the sort. You're going to marry me, Sancia, if I have to drag you to the Stato Civile by your hair.'

'That would cause a sensation,' she giggled feebly. 'You can't force me to say the words.'

'Can I not?' Spoken softly, but when she glanced up at him, his attitude had all the menace of a crouching tiger. 'Don't make me do something we may both regret,' he warned her. Then, with an obvious effort to speak reasonably, 'Be sensible, *cara*, we've gone too far to draw back now.'

'We haven't done anything irrevocable.'

'Not yet.'

Rick moved towards her and then the dam of his control broke. As he seized her by her shoulders his face became contorted with passion, his iron fingers biting into her flesh; she could feel the rage seething through him as he snarled:

'Do you think I'm going to allow you to make a fool of me, thwart all our plans, break Nonna's heart, just because you went where you shouldn't have gone and saw me with a girl? What do you propose to do?' He shook her until her teeth rattled. 'Go back to your loving father, or are you hankering after Timothy Bradley? There's nothing for you there, my girl. You're staying here with me, and liking it.'

But now her own temper had flared. She doubled her fists and pummelled his chest, crying, 'No, never! Let me go. I hate you!'

'Hate me as much as you please, but you'll do as I bid you.' He shifted his grip to enclose her in a crushing embrace as he started to kiss her, hard, punishing kisses that were meant to hurt . . . and did.

Sancia fought to free herself, turning her head this way and that to try to evade his mouth, anger stronger than the emotion he usually awoke in her. But he was far stronger than she was, and her resistance was futile.

He swung her up into his arms and carried her out of the *salotto* down the passage to his room. Bianca had not yet had time to do it, and the bed was unmade, his belongings strewn about everywhere. He was not a tidy man; the chamber reeked of his occupation. He let her slide to her feet while he locked the door, his intention only too plain. Sancia backed against the wall, her eyes wide with fright.

'Rick, you mustn't . . . you can't . . .'

'Can't I?'

Her dress was fastened by a long back zip and in one quick movement, he turned her round and drew it down. The garment slid to the floor, leaving her exposed in her bra and panties. Trembling, she crossed her hands over her breasts, while he tore off his shirt and flung it from him. Then he faced her, livid with passion, saying through gritted teeth:

'I've kept my hands off you out of respect for your innocence and because I thought you would not wish to anticipate our marriage, but I'll not permit you to play fast and loose with me. When I've finished with you, you'll be glad to marry me to make yourself respectable.'

Sancia threw up her head defiantly, green eyes flashing, 'Raping me won't alter my decision.'

His lips parted in a slow smile. 'But it will not be rape, *mia cara*, if you're willing.'

'Willing? Never!'

But against her will a creeping tide of excitement was rising.

In a last desperate attempt to escape, she tried to slip past him to the door, but he caught her round the waist in a cruel grip, and heaved her on to the tumbled bed. Momentarily the breath was knocked out of her, and before she could recover he was upon her, pulling her against the length of his hard lean body. He seemed to have checked his rage, for his hands were gentle as they moved over her. With sensuous deliberation he caressed her, stroking her back and hips. Lips and tongue trailed over her face and neck, lingering on her breasts, awaking every quivering nerve in response. He knew his power over her senses and was using it to subdue her rebellion. Slowly a dark tide of desire rose to meet his, and she was submerged by it. She arched her back to press closer to him, her arms creeping round his broad smooth shoulders, her fingers digging into his back. Mindless, she longed only for the culmination. He raised himself a little to draw her beneath him . . .

There was a loud knocking on the door.

'*Signor, signor, vengo presto! La Contessa è Svenuta!*'

At first the significance of the words did not penetrate his absorption, and Sancia was deaf to them, but as Bianca continued to bang on the door and cry out, Rick realised what she was saying. With an oath he sprang off the bed, and hurriedly resumed his clothes. Without a glance towards the girl lying on his bed, he unlocked the door and she heard the retreating fotsteps echo hollowly across the marble floors.

Slowly, through an agony of frustration, it penetrated her consciousness what had occurred. The Contessa had fainted—collapsed, perhaps was dying. Sancia struggled to her feet and mechanically reached for her dress, while waves of shame washed over her. How could she surrender so tamely to a man she hated and despised? But this was not the time to brood about that now; she wondered fearfully as she put on the dress Rick had stripped off her whether the Contessa was dead. She was fond of the old lady, but Rick was devoted to her with a selfless love that showed he did possess a heart.

If only . . . but this wasn't the time for vain regrets; she must find out what had happened. She tidied her tangled hair with Rick's brush and comb. Had Bianca known she was with him? The thought disturbed her until she reflected that Bianca would think it was quite natural if she was, since they were supposed to be engaged. Then she hurried from the room.

The doctor had been telephoned and Enrico sent flying in Rick's speedboat to fetch him. Bianca and Rick were trying to revive the old lady, and when Sancia appeared Rick snarled at her to keep out. She hung about, trying to comfort old Luigi and his wife who had made up their minds that their mistress was on the point of death. The doctor came, and Bianca joined them, describing dramatically how she had found the Contessa 'like one dead'. Sancia shut her up and set the staff to preparing a meal, for after all, they would have to eat. The doctor, a cheerful little man with a black beard, was with Rick for a long time in the *salotto* while he absorbed some of

Rick's Scotch whisky. When at last he had gone, Sancia ventured in and found him staring out of the window.

'How is she?' she asked shyly; she couldn't meet his eyes, not after what had occurred between them.

'Asleep,' he said curtly. 'It's been a bad attack; she may recover . . .' His voice faded.

'Is she going to hospital?'

'No. Dr Sforza thinks it's better not to move her. He's sending nurses.'

'Can I see her?'

'Later perhaps; at present she's sedated.' Rick turned towards her, his eyes coming alive in the pale mask of his face. Taking a step towards her, he demanded, 'You hadn't said anything to her about breaking our engagement?'

Sancia recoiled before the menace in his voice. 'Not a word.'

'I thought perhaps you had and that had brought on this attack.'

'Rick, I swear to you I hadn't.'

'Then don't you dare to do so, or I'll kill you. She must not be upset.'

'I wouldn't dream of doing so. I've got some sense!'

'Have you?' He didn't soften. 'Then you'd better put this on again.' He picked up her ring from where it still lay on the table. 'She'll notice at once if you're not wearing it.'

She eyed it reluctantly as he held it out to her, making no move to take it. Rick seized her hand and shoved it on to the appropriate finger. His touch made her shiver; whatever he was, whatever he did, she could never be indifferent to him. But what was she going to do now? She couldn't leave while her grandmother was so ill. Rick had turned back to contemplating the view out of the window. He said curtly, 'In view of Nonna's illness, our marriage will be postponed. But you will stay here until she is fully recovered. You understand?'

'I understand you're giving me orders,' she returned, rallying her drooping spirits. 'But I'll use my own discretion as to how far I'll obey them.'

He seemed on the verge of another outburst, but restrained himself. 'Need I point out that her life may depend upon your silence?'

'You needn't,' she said proudly. 'I'll keep up this . . . this farce as long as is necessary.'

She felt trapped.

CHAPTER EIGHT

Two days were to pass before Sancia was permitted to see her grandmother, days that seemed to creep by with leaden-footed slowness. Sisters from the convent of a nearby nursing order came to tend the Contessa day and night. They no longer wore the voluminous habit of former days and the stiff white coif, but midi-length black skirts, with veils over their heads. The doctor came and went; he and Rick spoke English together, probably so that the servants should not understand, and Sancia overheard him say, 'The difficulty is, *mio amico*, she seems to have lost the will to live.'

Sancia knew the old lady had a horror of losing her faculties; she often said she prayed she might go before that occurred. Now that she believed she had achieved her aim of a marriage between Rick and her grand-daughter it seemed she was ready to say her Nunc Dimittis.

During that period while the Contessa hovered between life and death, Sancia only saw Rick fleetingly. He dealt with numerous enquiries and business calls to Milan. There were visitors, elderly couples for the most part, bringing fruit and flowers, and he would call her to give them refreshments before they left. They accepted her as Rick's fiancée and the future mistress of the *palazzo* and added their felicitations to their condolences, which she received with the best grace she could, not always understanding what they were saying. The servants came to her for directions, though for the most part the household followed its usual routine. Bianca brought her meals on a tray, but she only picked at them. Where and when Rick ate she did not know; probably he went to the café in the *campo*, where he would find comfort with the black-haired girl. He refused to have anything cooked for him at home, which was a relief to Sancia who would have found formal meals with him an ordeal. He couldn't have shown her more plainly how little he needed her.

Sancia had ample time to consider her situation. She wore perforce his ring, not daring to take it off in case the Contessa summoned her. Rick had told her their marriage was only postponed, and apparently expected her to go through with it. But pride and jealousy would not allow her to concur. She could not marry him and accept the role of complaisant wife: moreover all her idealism, her delicate sensitivity, had been outraged by the despicable means he had used to force her to consent. She was desperately ashamed of the way she had responded. Her weakness humiliated her—she had betrayed all Martha's careful training, been as wanton as her mother. Yet she could not recall that morning without a quickening of her pulses, a stir of excitement in her stomach. Resolutely she pushed the memory away as too degrading to dwell upon.

When Nonna was better she must somehow get away, escape from the insidious enchantment of the Venetian scene, which had wrought such havoc in her father's life. He had sought to eradicate Lucia's part in her, and it was her mother's bad genes that were responsible for her abject surrender. Lucia had indulged her sensual nature, resulting in the loss of her husband and her child, and though Sancia had defended her, she knew the sequel had been tragic. Physically she still ached for Rick, his arms, his lips; mentally she rejected him. The conflict between the two sides of her nature tore her in two.

On the third evening, Rick came to her where she was sitting on the *salotto* balcony, listlessly watching the lights come on over the city, and she glanced at him nervously as he approached her. He was hollow-cheeked, and his eyes were sunken as if he had not been sleeping, but he was not unkempt. She had never seen him needing a shave. Dressed in black cords and shirt, he was a lean, dark figure in the gloaming and she was reminded again of Hamlet who had worn the shape of a skull about his neck. Involuntarily she shivered.

He noticed that. 'If you're cold, come inside,' he said shortly. Then more gently, 'She wants to see you, but she is very weak. Be careful what you say to her.'

Sancia looked up at him reproachfully. Was it possible he still believed she had precipitated the Contessa's heart attack by telling her she could not marry him?

'You can trust me!' she said indignantly.

'No need to get your hackles up,' he returned. 'I was only reminding you to control your tongue. *Va bene*, come along.'

He held out his hand to help her to rise from her seat, but she ignored it and brushed past him into the *salotto*, aware that he was following her as she made for the so-familiar room, like a black shadow of doom.

The Contessa seemed to have shrunk; her face looked tiny as she lay propped up against pillows in the huge bed. Her nose and chin had a pinched look that Sancia did not like, her small hands moving restlessly over the sheet, her eyes closed. Only the bedside lamp was on, and beyond its circle of light the vast room was dark. Sancia sat down on a chair beside the bed. Rick stood in the shadows, his back against the door, and was almost invisible, but Sancia was painfully conscious of his brooding presence.

Her grandmother opened her eyes and looked at her vaguely; recognising her, she smiled. 'Sancia . . .' Her voice was a mere thread. She stretched out her thin, white hand and Sancia took it in hers.

'*Carissima*, I'm so glad . . . you came to Venice . . .' She paused, and went on more strongly. 'You have fulfilled all my hopes, and now I can go in peace.'

'No,' Sancia whispered. 'You mustn't leave me.'

A slight negative movement of the white hand.

'Don't grieve . . . I go to join my loved ones.'

But *I* need you, *I* want you, was Sancia's unspoken cry; however, she had only known the Contessa for a short while, and she could not expect to mean as much to her as the ones she had lost.

The old woman did not speak again. Sancia wondered what Rick was thinking. Was he worrying that his plans might be brought to nothing by the Contessa's death? Then she rebuked herself for such thoughts at such a time.

There was a heavy silence in the room, broken only by the dying woman's troubled breathing. Rick was a motionless statue against the door, while Sancia tried to restrain her tears.

Suddenly the Contessa opened her eyes—she was gazing towards the shuttered window as if she saw a vision. For a fleeting moment Sancia glimpsed the lovely woman she had been in her youth—her dark eyes shone, her wrinkles seemed to disappear and her whole face was transfigured by an unearthly radiance.

'Leo!' she whispered, 'Lucia!'

Involuntarily Sancia glanced over her shoulder, half expecting to see someone there. Afterwards she was to recall that the Contessa had not called to Giovanni.

The radiance faded, the tired eyelids drooped over the dimming eyes.

'Go, *carissima*,' she murmured faintly. 'I must ... make my peace with God.'

Rick made a sign to someone Sancia had not previously noticed kneeling at the Contessa's prie-dieu in the dim recesses of the room. Noiselessly the nun rose and went to the door leading into the passage and opened it, the light outside revealed her veiled silhouette.

'*Avanti, padre.*'

Although a very indifferent Catholic all her life, the Contessa wanted to receive the last rites.

Feeling an interloper as the priest came in, Sancia crept into the *salotto* by the other door. There she sank weakly into a chair, the tension of the past three days taking its toll. The twilight had deepened but she made no move to turn on the lights. From behind the closed door of the bedroom came the faint drone of voices, and she felt more than ever isolated. She sat there for a long time, without thought. Dusk turned to night, occasional flashes of light crossed the high ceiling from some passing craft. From the Contessa's room there was now no sound.

Then the door opened and Rick came in, closing it behind him, and flicked on the lights. Seeing her, he exclaimed, 'All alone in the dark!'

Sancia blinked at him dazedly; their eyes met. His were dark, unfathomable, his face expressionless, but she knew.

'She's gone, hasn't she?' she asked tonelessly.

He bowed his head. 'She made a good end.'

Like a desolate child, Sancia cried, 'Now I'm alone in the world!'

A muscle twitched in his cheek, but his eyes remained stony as he returned, 'You have a choice.'

But she hadn't, not after what she had seen on the *campo* and the way he had treated her when she had tried to break her engagement. She deserved better than to be his second string, an instrument to assuage his desire when his true love was unavailable, she told herself fiercely. She struggled to her feet.

'I ... I'll go upstairs.'

She staggered as she tried to cross the room. Instantly Rick was beside her, his strong arm about her waist, supporting her. She leaned against him, forgetting everything but the joy of being close to his lean, hard body, the contact for which she had yearned. His arm tightened as he said gently, '*Amore mia*, you're all in. You'd better sit down again.'

If only she was his love—but she didn't want any more pretence. As he guided her back to her chair she looked wistfully up into his dark face above her own, and it flashed into her mind that their mutual grief might forge a link to draw them together, for his expression had softened, but the brief hope was quickly dispelled as he said meditatively, 'The *palazzo* will be yours now.'

Sancia was shocked that he could mention such a subject at such a moment. Was his love for Nonna as phoney as his feelings for herself. He was obsessed by the place, and it must be hitting him hard to realise he might be about to lose it. The arm about her waist held her possessively, but it was not her he wanted to possess. She said in a low, tense voice, 'I don't want it. You can have it.'

'Don't be silly. It's your heritage.'

'But I don't, I never have wanted it!' Her voice rose hysterically, and she threw off his arm with a violent movement. 'And I won't marry you. You're callous to talk about it now. No, don't dare to touch me . . .' She retreated as he made a movement towards her. 'I can't bear to feel your hands upon me after . . . after . . .' She choked over the lie, for though she despised him for his avarice, his ruthless pursuit of his objective, his disregard of her own feelings, she longed to throw herself into his arms and beg him to love and comfort her.

For a second a devil looked out of his eyes and she recoiled, expecting another onslaught, but he mastered himself, thrusting his hands into his trouser pockets and walking to the window. Sancia stood trembling in the tense pause that followed, then with his back towards her he said quietly, 'You're perfectly free, Sancia.'

He came back to the table, where, as was usual, a decanter and glasses were set out, and poured a glass of wine.

'Drink this,' he bade her, coming towards her. 'You need it.'

Mechanically she took it, glancing timidly up at him, and saw there was no softness in his face and his eyes were smouldering; he was controlling his anger with difficulty. He was furious because she had failed to succumb to his charms. Acting upon a sudden furious impulse, she threw the wine into his impassive face and rushed from the *salotto*, terrified of his reaction to what she had done. Behind the locked door of her own room, she dropped on her bed in a storm of tears, weeping as much for what might have been and was not, as for her grandmother.

The Contessa was interred with all the pomp and circumstance of former days. A fleet of black-draped gondolas conveyed her to the city's cemetery on the twin

cypress-clad islands, to lie in the Rossini mausoleum
beside her first husband and her daughter.

Sancia was glad to find she was not expected to attend.
Rick had hardly spoken to her since the scene in the
salotto, only when it was absolutely necessary, and he
kept his eyes averted. She stood on her balcony watching
the cavalcade float down the Grand Canal, the sable-clad
gondoliers wielding their oars, on their way to cross the
lagoon. She felt numb, but now it was all over she must
try to shake off her inertia and face her future. So much
had happened in such a short time, causing her lethargy,
but she must shake it off and become active. Rick would
have to return to Milan almost at once, his presence
would be needed there, and presumably she could stay in
Venice until she had made her plans. She would contact
Judy, who had written that so far she had failed to find a
congenial flatmate and would welcome her. Somehow
she must dispose of all the expensive clothes that had
been bought for her; perhaps the shops would take back
those she had not worn. Lastly she must inform Rick of
her intentions, and that would require courage. She had
taken off her ring—there was no need to wear that any
longer, and if Rick didn't offer to pay her fare home, she
would have to sell or pawn it to obtain the money, though
it wasn't, strictly speaking, hers. But she didn't think he
would make any objections, once the little matter of the
palazzo was settled. Little matter? Sancia smiled wanly;
it had figured largely throughout her stay in Venice.

If the Contessa *had* left it to her, Rick would be sure to
want to buy it from her. She knew he had long tried to
persuade her grandmother to sell it to him, it was such an
obvious solution, but the old woman had obstinately
refused to part with what she called 'the Rossini
inheritance'. Though Sancia suspected he had often

helped the two women financially, he could not be expected to spend money on restoring a property which the unpredictable Lucia might dispose of elsewhere. He was a hard-headed businessman, and Lucia might have wanted to spite him. Sancia did not know what his real relationship with her mother had been. He had expressed admiration for her beauty, but deplored her conduct, which he had tried to conceal from Nonna, and probably Lucia had resented his chauvinistic attitude. When Lucia had predeceased her, the Contessa had become obsessed with the idea of a union between the two people who had a claim on her, which would solve everything so conveniently, and Rick had dissembled and betrayed his real love to fall in with her wishes.

Sancia found she was loath to take money from Rick, although being in a dilapidated condition and probably mortgaged, the palace could not be worth a great deal. She would prefer to make it over to him by Deed of Gift, but his pride might not want to accept it. However, she would be in a position to dictate terms, and that thought gave her a fleeting satisfaction. Once the matter was settled one way or another, she was sure he would be glad to be rid of her, and would quickly forget her, she thought sadly, stifling the ache in her heart.

The last gondola disappeared into the misty distance, and a water-bus came from the opposite direction with a crowd of noisy youngsters aboard, dispelling the fantasy of past glories with its bustling modernity. Sancia sighed and turned back into the room. She prayed Nonna would rest in peace. Her world had ceased to exist, and Sancia's was not hers.

Beppo was lying on her bed and she sat down beside him, stroking his ears. He wasn't supposed to be there—Bianca would grumble that he left hairs—but she had brought him up for company. If she took him back with her, he would have to go into quarantine, but she didn't trust the *palazzo* staff to look after him, and Rick would want to get rid of him. Quarantine was a better fate than being left to starve in Venice.

'We've a grim six months ahead of us,' she told him, 'but we'll have a glad reunion at the end of them.'

But after she had left, she would never see Riccardo Antonelli again.

On the following day the Notary was expected with the Contessa's will. Sancia again took refuge in her room, where to avoid Rick she spent most of her time. She did not want to be present, looking like an expectant heiress, she thought resentfully, and surely Rick could cope alone. But he had other ideas.

The imperious knock on her door caused her to jump, and he called to her, 'Are you there? I want to speak to you.'

The sound of his voice caused her heart to knock, as she asked, 'What about?'

She looked anxiously at the door, which she hadn't locked, and at Beppo again on her bed.

'Are you resting?'

'No. Yes! Please leave me alone.'

'I can't talk with a door between us.' Impatiently he turned the handle and came into the room. He wore a black suit with a black tie knotted at his throat, very formal, very correct and looking most distinguished. Sancia was in white; the Contessa's 'trousseau' contained no mourning garments. The halter-neck sun-dress displayed her sun-tanned arms and shoulders, and her legs were bare above her sandals. Her hair was loose upon her shoulders, and she looked fragile; her recent traumas had put dark marks beneath her eyes which seemed to increase their size. They widened in alarm as she beheld him. What did he want?

'You needn't look so scared!' he exclaimed irritably. 'I've no evil intentions. I merely want to tell you the Notary is due in half an hour and you must be present.'

'Must I?'

'Of course. There are many things to settle which concern you.' His eyes ran over her critcally. 'Haven't you a black dress?'

Sancia swallowed convulsively. 'Only an evening one.'

The gown she had worn on their first date, so long ago it seemed—that enchanted evening by the river when Rick had decided she was 'presentable'. If only she had known what was in his mind then, she would have died before she accepted his invitation. She recalled that he had said their fates were linked, so perhaps what had happened was inevitable. If she had refused he would have found some other means of contacting her, for when he had a purpose, he was ruthless in pursuit of it, and she, poor stooge, unaware of his calculated motives, had fallen for him. But possibly that was inevitable too. Rick caught sight of Beppo, another fool, for he wagged an ingratiating tail.

'What the devil is that beast doing here?'

'He ... comforts me,' Sancia said lamely, 'he's company.'

His carved lips curled. She had never noticed before what a cruel twist they had. 'You prefer a dog's society to mine?'

Which, she might have reminded him, had not been offered, but since she had thrown the wine in his face, she could hardly blame him.

'Infinitely,' she retorted.

He turned away from her and looked at his watch.

'*Ecco*, you have twenty-five minutes in which to make yourself look respectable.' He swung round, his eyes going to her bare shoulders, lingering there, with an avid look. Instinctively she caught up her make-up cape which she had dropped on a nearby chair and covered her small breasts. So, desire wasn't quite dead, but wasn't that his natural reaction to any pretty woman?

Rick laughed scornfully at her action, and his eyes became expressionless, as she said pointedly, 'If I'm to change you'd better go. You shouldn't be here anyway.'

'Fouling your virginal nest?' Again he laughed. 'My apologies,' now he was mocking, 'but you're so elusive I wanted to be sure you got the message. You'll come down?'

'I suppose so.'

'If you don't, I'll come and fetch you, and it's no use locking your door. Luigi has a master key.'

'Oh, I'll be there,' she promised hastily, scared by the hint of a threat in his voice. 'There'll be no need for any more caveman stuff.'

She thought he winced, but wasn't sure.

'Normally I'm quite a mild man,' he remarked, and Sancia could have laughed in her turn with derision. That was an adjective that could never be applied to him. Rick shot her a sly glance. 'I'm only dangerous when provoked.'

Which meant, don't dare to oppose me.

'I said I'd come down,' she said dully, 'and I'll change my dress.'

'Good girl.' He started for the door but paused by her bed.

Beppo, to her surprise, stood up and tried to lick his hand. Dogs usually knew who liked them.

Rick patted his head. 'Take good care of your

mistress,' he told the animal. 'You're privileged.'

He went out of the room, closing the door softly behind him while Sancia stared after him, amazed by his final words. Privileged to look after her? But when had Rick ever implied that he wished to do so? He had shown scant regard for her welfare.

She rummaged through her wardrobe and found a dark silk dress that she had never worn. It had a pleated midi skirt, and long transparent sleeves. She vaguely remembered buying it, and it was very nearly black though it had some gold trimming on the bodice. That could be concealed by a nylon scarf. She put it on, and scraped her hair back from her face, rolling it into a knot in her nape. Black strap sandals completed her outfit, though she didn't bother with tights. The skirt was long enough to conceal most of her legs. A dusting of powder increased her pallor, and she used no other make-up. Her appearance, she thought, should satisfy him; too bad if it didn't, she didn't care.

The light caught the ring glittering on her dressing-table. No, that she would not wear, hadn't he said she was free? But she could never be wholly free from the impression he had made upon her. No other man . . . 'Oh, damn him,' she ejaculated aloud. 'I'm being maudlin. Of course I'll get over him. I must.'

Calling to Beppo, she left the room.

The Notary was a dark little man with a beard and a balding scalp, stout too, the sort of man she had imagined Gio would turn out to be before Rick appeared. When Sancia came in, he stood up, bowing politely as Rick introduced them, and Rick pulled out a chair for her. The polished table was strewn with papers, and she was seated on one of the high dining chairs opposite to the two men.

The Notary began; 'Now zat ze Signorina Everardo 'as come, we will proceed wiz ze will of ze Signora Antonelli,' (he gave her her correct title) 'formerly ze Contessa Rossini.'

He spoke English for Sancia's benefit, but with a heavy accent. It was, he explained, a new will made only recently. There were small bequests to the servants; the Signora had not many assets, she had been living on capital. To Sancia she left her mother's jewellery, of which only a few of the good pieces were left, and to Giovanni Riccardo Antonelli she left the *palazzo* and all its contents, for she believed the husband should own the roof-tree of the home, and she hoped he would do his best to preserve it. She wished him and his wife a long and happy life beneath it. She did not mention the wife's name.

Sancia received the information with thankfulness. Now there need be no buying and selling, no Deeds of Gift. Rick had been left what was in reality his birthright, for the *palazzo* would have fallen to pieces long ago but for the elder Antonelli's money. They could ignore the Contessa's expectation that they would marry, for the dead had no right to seek to influence the living.

She glanced surreptitiously at Rick, expecting to see relief and triumph in his face, but instead he was regarding her thoughtfully with a puckered brow. Surely he didn't feel he was in any way bound to fulfil Nonna's wishes? He hadn't shown himself over-scrupulous up to now. Well, if he did, she would soon persuade him otherwise. In spite of her mother, she was a British girl with an English surname and Italy was not her country; lovely as the *palazzo* was, she had never felt she had any right to it.

The Notary congratulated Rick and they plunged into

Italian, doubtless discussing details he found difficult to translate. When there was a slight pause, Sancia asked if she might be excused, as her presence was no longer needed. Rick nodded absently, but the Notary sprang to his feet and shook her hand.

'My felicitations, *signorina*.'

She smiled, blushed, but said nothing. He would soon learn that the marriage was off. She would take Beppo for a walk along the Molo and on her return, ring up Judy to advise her of her coming.

CHAPTER NINE

SANCIA returned from her walk by the back alleys. The yard behind the house contained one lovely thing, a wisteria that grew up one side of it. For the rest, it was a jumble of fallen masonry, cases and old cartons. Rick had plans to re-pave it and make it into a miniature Spanish patio with hanging potted plants. She had heard him discuss it with the Contessa. She felt an unexpected pang, for she would never see what he made of it.

Beppo's kennel was in one corner, but he rarely occupied it, being more often in the kitchen, where the servants tolerated him, or with her. Now he decided to go into it. Removing his muzzle, which in common with other dogs he wore more often as an ornament about his neck than over his face, Sancia turned to ascend the short flight of steps going up to the kitchen door, when Rick appeared at the top of them. He had exchanged his jacket and tie for one of his favourite black pullovers, a thin one that clung to his muscular figure. Hands in trouser pockets, he lounged against the door jamb, surveying her lazily.

Sancia too had changed, into slacks and a flowered top. She looked very young and boyish among the debris of the yard, and she was conscious that she had done two things of which he disapproved: put on trousers and gone out on her own, then she remembered that she was free. She didn't have to try to please him any more.

'May I come up?' she asked, for he was barring her way.

'Your pardon, *signorina*.' His face changed to mockery. He jumped lightly to the ground, not using the steps, and stood beside her. 'The way is clear, but don't go rushing upstairs to your virginal retreat. I've matters to discuss with you.'

She threw him a nervous glance—she distrusted this mood—but she was glad to see he was recovering his spirits after the last distressing days. She said lightly, 'I thought business was over for the day.'

Beppo left his kennel and came fawning up to Rick.

'There, now!' she exclaimed reproachfully. 'You've woken him up, and I thought he was settled for a while.'

'As you thought I was too.' He grinned at her, a flash of white teeth in his brown face. 'He can come along, he won't interfere with our . . . discourse.'

She slowly climbed the steps, aware he was close behind her. In silence they traversed the passages and stairs leading to the *salotto*. The papers had disappeared from the dining table, and he indicated one of the armchairs before the empty fireplace.

'Sit down, make yourself comfortable.'

She obeyed, crossing her long legs, but she didn't feel comfortable, she rarely was in his company. Stimulated, angry, anxious, but not comfortable—he was too disturbing for that.

'A drink?' he suggested, 'or shall I ring for tea?'

'I don't want anything,' she returned quickly, 'let's get it over.'

'How charmingly you put things!' He sat down on a sofa opposite her, and dropped his bantering manner. 'It's your future I'm concerned about. Nonna has made no provision for you, believing of course that we would marry, but now you say you've changed your mind . . .?' He paused, letting his words hang upon the air.

'Oh, I can manage,' she said hurriedly. 'I'll go back to England, of course, as soon as it can be arranged.'

Rick said nothing, and she began to twist her handkerchief between nervous fingers. 'You said I was free.'

'Perfectly free, I've no intention of trying to . . . er . . . coerce you,' he told her pleasantly. 'But freedom can be very expensive, and I thought you might be having second thoughts.'

'About mar . . . marrying you? But it's not necessary now. You've got the *palazzo*, which . . .' a note of bitterness crept into her voice, 'was to have been my dowry. I've nothing else to offer you.'

'Haven't you?' He gave her a peculiar look. 'Your grandmother expected we would marry when she changed her will. You are Lucia's daughter and she always regarded the house as her heritage. You are the only descendant of the Rossinis left.'

Sancia made an impatient gesture. 'All that means nothing to me.'

'It should do.'

'I said it doesn't and I also told you, as you've just remarked, that I've changed my mind.'

She had never expected that Rick would still contemplate marrying her, now he had got what he wanted without.

'A woman's privilege,' he observed, 'and you could change it again.'

There was a short silence, while he scanned her drooping face, and her fingers began to tear the delicate fabric between them, as she wondered how she could convince him that she meant what she said.

Rick said quietly, 'The truth is you can't forgive me for what I did that morning.'

Rich colour flooded her face as she shook her head, but it was herself she couldn't forgive for her abject surrender.

'You were so . . . so brutal,' she flung at him.

'You'd given me a shock, and I forgot myself. I'm only human, Sancia.'

It was as near to an apology as she would ever receive from him.

'Let's forget it,' she said magnanimously, well knowing she never could.

He took out one of his cheroots and lit one, while he regarded her sombrely. Again memory flashed back: a dim conservatory, a sinister stranger, her first stirrings of what she now knew had been desire—but then she had been high on witches' brew and didn't realise what was happening. She had no premonition of the baneful influence she was admitting into her life.

Through an ascending spiral of smoke, he accused her.

'It would apear that you accidentally saw me with a girl, a mere child, in what you considered to be compromising circumstances. Is that sufficient reason to break off what promised to be a most satisfactory union?'

Sancia raised stormy eyes to his cool grey ones.

'Who was she?'

'That I can't tell you.'

'Another charade?' She laughed scornfully. 'You do love mysteries, don't you, Rick? But whoever she was, I heard you tell her your marriage would make no difference to your relationship with her. It was bad enough to be marrying a man who didn't love me . . .' He made a movement of protest, but she rushed on '. . . but still worse when I discovered he loves someone else, and you needn't try to pretend otherwise; I'm sure I don't know why you should, now I know the truth.'

She saw the flash of anger in his eyes and knew she was on dangerous ground, but she didn't flinch.

'Eavesdroppers often get a wrong impression,' he told her caustically, 'but be that as it may, I don't like being spied upon.'

'No, you preserve the right of espionage to yourself,' she said tartly, for his initial approach to her in disguise had never ceased to rankle. 'But don't let us quarrel, Rick, you've got the *palazzo*, and ... and Nonna has gone.' Her voice shook, then, recovering, she concluded: 'It can only be your vanity that's hurt because I wish to leave.'

'Or yours because I won't grovel at your feet and beg you to stay,' he retorted. 'That isn't my way.'

He stood up and walked to the window, and her eyes followed him yearningly. Only pride restrained her from crying out that she would stay with him always under any conditions, but she couldn't see any real happiness for either of them in such a future, he with his mind always on other things, and she growing bitter and resentful. She supposed he felt some obligation to marry her because it was the Contessa's wish, but she didn't want to be considered an obligation, she wanted ... Oh, what was the use of repining? What she wanted had been given elsewhere.

Rick ground out his cheroot and flung the stub into the canal through the open window, an action she deplored. Then he came back to stand in front of her.

'It's senseless to bicker about what can't be helped, but I feel responsible for you, *mia cara*.' Both face and voice had softened. 'You'd much better marry me, you will then be assured of a good home ...'

'A meal ticket?' she cut in. 'I earned my living before, and I can again.'

He smiled sardonically. 'A dreary prospect. I admire your independent spirit, but consider. Your father has married again, your friend ...' He shrugged his shoulders. 'I shouldn't think she's too reliable, neither do I think you're cut out to be a career girl. You're too soft to be competitive, and *Dio mio*, no one knows better than I how tough the rat race can be. I can give you security...' He hesitated, then continued, 'If I promise not to insist upon my ... er ... conjugal rights, won't you reconsider?'

Sancia stared at him in blank astonishment. Recollecting his passionate lovemaking on more than one occasion, she could only surmise that his fancy for her had evaporated. He seemed to be genuinely concerned for her welfare, and that touched her. What he had said about her future in England was only too true, and she would not enjoy having to tell her father that her marriage had fallen through, or face Judy's condolences for failing to keep her man, for that was how she would look at it. She might well have difficulty in finding another job in the present climate, and to hang around Judy's flat existing on unemployment benefit was not a cheery prospect.

Rick went on, 'As you know, my work is in Milano. Under these changed circumstances, I shall rent a flat there and only look in here occasionally to preserve appearances.'

'Isn't this your home?'

'I have no settled home. I came here to see Nonna, and sometimes it was a drag. It was her home and Lucia's.'

'Then won't you want to sell the *palazzo*?'

'Certainly not. When it's renovated it will be a

valuable asset. You can help me by keeping an eye on the
workmen and superintending redecorations. It'll be an
occupation for you.'

Sancia was dumbfounded. All his manoeuvring to gain
possession of the place, and now he was calmly
suggesting she should live in it on her own, a grass widow
without a real husband; it sounded like a fantasy. She
couldn't take it in.

'If you find it too big, you could move into a smaller
house, and when it's finished we might make it into a
show-place for tourists. You should have someone to live
with you. Perhaps Miss Vincent would like to come
here.' He smiled. 'Enrico misses her, and I would pay her
a companion's salary.'

'But ... but ...' Sancia was bewildered. He was
offering her so much for no return. Could this quiet,
impassive man be the same person as the one who had
embraced her so fiercely when she had said she would not
marry him? He looked completely uninvolved; only his
eyes were watchful, the same close scrutiny with which
she was so familiar.

'But what? Don't you trust me? I swear to you, Sancia,
I'll not lay a finger on you, and though the Antonellis
can't boast of titled ancestors like the Rossinis, they
always keep their word.'

'Of course I trust you,' she said quickly, wondering if
she could. Once they were wed she would be entirely at
his disposal. 'You've made me an incredibly generous
offer, Rick, but why should you?'

'Must I keep repeating that Nonna meant this to be
your home?' he told her patiently. 'She'd come back and
haunt me if I turned you out!'

She was more and more amazed. She had never

expected that Rick would give such consideration to the wishes of others.

'Perhaps I could live here temporarily, without——' she began hesitantly, and he cut her short.

'You certainly could not! Your position would be far too ambiguous. You'll need the protection of my name, for although you won't be sharing my bed, it'll be believed that you do.'

Sancia blushed fierily and looked at the torn remnants of her handkerchief between her fingers. If Rick wanted her as a wife she couldn't continue to deny him when he was prepared to give her security, a home and his name. After all, what had she against him? An affair with another woman, resentment against his deception? Against the magnitude of his generosity they seemed paltry affronts, and she became aware of an increasing longing to be in his arms. This talk of rare visits, his flat in Milan, and not sharing his bed was like so many douches of cold water. But did he still want her?

She said tentatively, 'It doesn't seem fair, I mean . . . you're depriving yourself . . .' She stopped, wondering how to put it.

Rick's fine mouth curled sardonically.

'You needn't worry about that. I shan't be depriving myself of anything. Though you may shrink from my embraces, there are plenty of others who will welcome them.'

Sancia froze. She knew of at least one—were there others in Milan? She was flattering herself to imagine he still desired her after she had rejected him. But his words had evoked another train of thought. Though she was quite convinced she would never love another man, Rick ought to have a real wife, to give him heirs.

'But suppose . . . later on, one of us wants to marry someone else?'

His black brows drew together and his grey glance pierced her, as he asked dangerously, 'Have you someone else in mind?'

'No one at all.'

'Not?' He clenched his fists. 'Tim Bradley?'

She laughed; poor Tim, she hadn't given him a thought for months.

'I'm as likely to want to marry Tim as you are to marry Paula.'

His face cleared as he relaxed. 'Then that's okay, and if you don't know, let me tell you an unconsummated marriage can easily be annulled.'

The same thought occurred to both of them, and he gave her a lopsided grin as she smiled uncertainly.

'It didn't happen, fortunately, you're still *virgo intacta*.'

Suddenly she wished she wasn't, that what he had meant to do had been completed. That would have ended all her uncertainties, she would have felt that she belonged to him irrevocably, for good or ill. She suspected that he had had that in mind when he tried to take her, though for a very different reason. Now he was saying it was fortunate because it left a way out, and she could be very sure he would keep his word, for he wouldn't want to cut off the means of retreat if they found their arrangement didn't work. That thought ought to have been reassuring, but she found it depressing.

With a hint of impatience, Rick asked with some of his old arrogance, '*Dio mio*, can't you make up your mind? You've a great deal to gain and nothing to lose if you agree.'

'I . . . I realise that, and I'm awfully grateful . . . but

please give me a little time to think it over.'

'You always did think too much,' he complained. 'If you must think, think of the alternative, a father and a stepmother who don't want you, probable unemployment, the London murk . . .' he glanced at the sunlight pouring through the window, and concluded softly, 'Venezia is a beautiful city, Sancia, and the *palazzo* needs a mistress.'

When she was alone in her room, Sancia endeavoured to assemble her confused thoughts and consider Rick's proposal dispassionately. If she accepted it, the material advantages to her were immense, but she was bewildered by the new image Rick had presented, and found herself seeking for an ulterior motive. Hitherto she had come to regard him as a selfish, despotic man, who went all out to get what he wanted, trampling on any who got in his way, his only soft spot his affection for the old woman, who was not in fact a relation at all, and that had been suspect because he hoped she would leave him the *palazzo*. She wondered what his parents had been like—the English mother, of whom, the Contessa had let slip, his grandfather had not approved, having a more advantageous match in view for his only son. But Rick's father had gone his own way, as all the Antonellis did, being forceful men. Luckily Giovanni had died before he could affect his grandson's destiny, but not before he had succeeded in driving Lucia Rossini from her home. Rick had seemed equally ruthless, determined to acquire the *palazzo* and seeing in herself the easiest way to attain it. When she had rebelled he had deliberately used his power over her senses to break her resistance, although his heart was involved elsewhere. All this fitted the character she had attributed to him, but now, with the *palazzo* in his possession, when he had no need to consider her further, he had shown her a totally different side to his nature. He seemed genuinely concerned about her future and was anxious to carry out the Contessa's wishes to the extent of offering her a marriage in name only.

If she hadn't witnessed that emotional scene in the *campo* she might have believed he still desired her, and she was sure that in time she would be unable to resist him, when she had got over her pique, but the words she had overheard continually haunted her. 'It will make no difference, everything will be as it was before,'—with a ring of sincerity in his voice. A child, he had called the unknown, but she was no child. She had clung to him with all a woman's passion, and Italian girls matured young. He was prepared to make Sancia mistress of the *palazzo*, but now there was no risk of Nonna discovering his illicit liaison, he would openly seek his sexual satisfaction elsewhere.

Could she manage to live in Rick's house, which had begun to feel more like her home than her father's house had ever done, on a fraternal basis, while her awakened senses still craved for him? But she would only see him infrequently, he had made that clear, and she would have the pleasure of helping to restore the old palace in the drowning city that she had come to love, all the more deeply for the danger that it might disappear for ever. She would be spared the humiliation of being regarded as jilted, for that was what her father and Judy would think. Last but not least there was Beppo, with the threat of a long quarantine in front of him.

In time she would regain her cool aloofness, for she had not been fully initiated, and what she had never had she would not miss. She might even be able to feel indifferent to Rick's other attachments. If she could school herself to be always gracious, poised and tolerant when they met, he might—just might—come to love her.

It would not be easy, but she could do it, and it was better, far better, than to be separated from Rick for ever. For one thing did emerge from her meditations, the fact that in spite of all that had happened, he was the most important person in her life.

Rick was leaving for Milan early the next morning, but that night he decided they would dine together. It was the first time since Nonna's sudden illness that they were to have a formal meal in the *salotto*. The servants were pleased by this return to normality; they had mourned their mistress with extravagant Latin lamentations, which Sancia had tried to calm, but like all their volatile emotions, they quickly faded.

Sancia put on her black dress, the one she had worn on her first date with Rick, and wondered if he would remember it. This time she did make-up more elaborately, adding blusher to her pale cheeks. She was delighted that Rick was staying in, she had half expected he would have had an assignation elsewhere—that girl was ever in her thoughts. She reflected that although he might plan to visit the *palazzo* infrequently, that was not to say he could not come to Venice unknown to her, or even transport his young woman to his flat in Milan. But she had decided to marry him on his own terms, and she must do her best to ignore the existence of other women.

When she entered the *salotto* she saw with a pang that the table was laid with the red Murano glasses heavily encrusted with gold, which only appeared on special occasions. Rick must have ordered them. The Contessa had loved what she called a '*festa*' and jumped at any excuse for a celebration. The last time had been when Sancia and Rick became engaged. Judy had been there then and Enrico had been included to increase the male element, for his status was higher than that of a servant. Now, alas, the Contessa's chair was vacant.

The chandeliers poured light down upon the polished table and silverware, the red roses in a crystal bowl, all being reflected in the mirrors so that the room glittered with red and gold. Shone also on Rick's smooth black hair and Sancia's own burnished head.

He was wearing informal evening dress, a white silk shirt and black trousers with, the night being hot, one of the new embroidered waistcoats. Looking at his dress and noticing a bottle of champagne in ice, Sancia realised he meant this to be an occasion. He was so certain she had made her decision in his favour.

Perversely she felt inclined to decline his offer, but common sense prevailed. Rick was Rick, a man who never admitted defeat; hadn't he won all along the line? She would only be spiting herself if she refused him.

'How charming you look,' he told her as they sat down to eat, the urbane charmer once more. 'The jewellery you've inherited isn't up to much. A diamond necklace would look well with that dress. I must get you one.'

'Oh no, Rick, please. You're giving me far too much as it is.'

He gave her a slanted look.

'My wife must be suitably adorned.'

So he was taking her consent for granted, and the idea of being used as a display case for the jewels he bought to impress his friends did not appeal to her.

'I haven't said yes yet,' she reminded him.

'You'll be a fool if you don't,' he returned, and gave all his attention to the excellent lasagne Bianca had brought in.

Sancia kept her temper with difficulty.

'But I shan't be entertaining,' she began.

'Of course you will, after a decent period of mourning. Nonna's friends will come to call, and I may bring business colleagues occasionally to dine and sleep. When the *palazzo* is refurbished, I shall want to show off my beautiful wife and my ... er ... country residence.'

She noticed he had balked at saying 'home'. Home, it was said, was where the heart was, but his would not be with her.

'That's rather a daunting prospect,' said Sancia slowly.

'Nonsense, you'll be equal to it, and you'll have that ebullient friend of yours to support you. She'd tackle anything.'

'Judy may not want to come.'

'She will,' he returned confidently, 'if only to renew her acquaintance with Enrico. They correspond, did you know?'

She hadn't known, and was astonished. Judy had never mentioned it.

'But how ... I mean, the language difficulty?'

'I've been helping him with his English.'

Sancia was again amazed. That Rick had been giving up his precious time to assist one of his dependants.

'He'll have to do his Army Service soon,' Rick went on. 'It was deferred because ... Nonna ...' he paused as he uttered her name, 'needed him. He's a bright lad, he might make the army his career if I can get him commissioned. She could do a lot worse.'

Matchmaking seemed to run in the family, Sancia thought, but Rick's efforts were more promisng than his grandfather's had been.

'You seem to have got it all cut and dried,' she observed. 'He ought to be grateful to you.'

'Gratitude is the rarest of human virtues,' he said

cynically. 'So I don't expect it.'

Bianca came in to change the courses; escalopes of veal followed the lasagne.

'Now to our affairs,' said Rick when she had gone. 'There's no reason for delay, and the sooner your position is regularised the better. Say, in a fortnight's time?'

Again Sancia had the sensation of being rushed off her feet.

'But . . . but we're in mourning.'

'There'll only be ourselves, we won't advertise it. Incidentally, the workmen will be starting next week; they'll try not to inconvenience you. You can begin looking at furniture and materials. Spend as much as you please, money's no object.'

She said diffidently, 'Suppose you don't like what I choose?'

'I'm sure I will. I've every confidence in your good taste.'

Sancia felt immensely gratified. It would be delightful to do over the house according to her own ideas. She would do her very best to please him, and she knew vaguely the sort of thing he would admire.

'What colours would you suggest for this room?' he went on, and Sancia was drawn into discussing the decorations. Ice cream and cheese followed the veal. Rick opened the champagne and poured the bubbling liquid into her glass, and then his.

'To the *palazzo*!' he said, raising the red and gold goblet, 'and may you be happy in it.'

Sancia looked at him over the rim of hers.

'But Rick, I still haven't said yes.'

He smiled at her. 'Wasn't that a foregone conclusion, *mia cara*?'

Remembering what they had been discussing, she supposed it was.

When they came to say goodnight, he told her he would not see her in the morning, as he was making a very early start.

'So I'll say goodbye now. *Arrivederci, mia cara.*'

They were standing facing each other, and a wave of love and longing swept over her. He had been so unexpectedly kind and thoughtful, for she realised that the talk about the renovations had been intended to distract her from her grief. He too had been aware of that empty chair. He looked so handsome standing under the light spilling from the chandelier, the lines of strain that had marked his face during the last few days at last erased. Her husband-to-be, who had denied her his bed. Was it too late? Couldn't she eradicate, temporarily at least, the image of the black-haired girl? Impulsively she moved towards him, holding out her hand.

'Rick . . .'

For a second, flame flickered in his eyes, and he took a step towards her. Sancia's heart leaped, he did still want her, he was going to take her in his arms. She forgot her reservations, her doubts and fears, even her jealousy, wanting only to be held against him, to feel his mouth on hers, to be taken to his bed. This time she would yield to him with rapture.

But as the thoughts flickered through her mind, he drew back. The light in his eyes was extinguished; they were as cold as a wintry sea. Ignoring her outstretched hand, he drew his heels together and bowed formally.

'Goodnight again, *mia cara.*' He smiled faintly, perhaps recalling her first attempt to speak his tongue. '*Ciao*'.

Her hand dropped to her side as she returned

automatically, 'Goodnight, and a safe journey.'

He had promised he would not touch her and he was keeping his word.

While a despairing protest hovered on her lips, Rick went with alacrity to open the door for her as if he was anxious for her to be gone. He wanted her to go before ... before what? Perhaps she had only imagined that split second when he had looked at her with desire. She hurried past him and blindly groped her way upstairs, brushing away her stinging tears.

CHAPTER TEN

SANCIA and Judy sat before a log fire in the refurbished *salotto*. The tarnished mirrors had been fitted with new glass and Sancia herself had re-gilded the frames. The heavy, shabby furniture had been replaced by lighter pieces, and a modern suite couch and armchairs had been covered in green velour, with a green and gold carpet fitted over the marble floor. A television set had been installed—the Contessa had always refused to have one, regarding it as an invention of the devil. Winter in Venice was warmer than in England, but there were often wet, damp days when a fire was welcome. Work on the *casa* was far from finished—there was scaffolding outside—but Sancia had completed the rooms on the first floor, and the kitchen had been modernised. Sancia had been too busy searching for the right materials and furniture to indulge in her secret heartache. Rick came and went and to her relief approved the innovations, but he was always impersonal and aloof. The architect had shaken his head over the foundations—the inroads of the Adriatic, the wash of the *vaporetti* was slowly undermining the ancient palaces—but he would do all he could to preserve the building as long as possible.

'It should outlast our lifetime,' Rick had remarked cheerfully, and Sancia had reflected with a dart of pain that under their present arrangement there could be none to come after them.

Judy had been pleased to come and live with her, and was half engaged to Enrico, who was doing his belated

military service and came back on leave occasionally, a
handsome, dashing young soldier.

Sancia had asked tentatively if he knew of Judy's past,
and her friend had told her without embarrassment, 'He
knows I'm not a virgin, if that's what you mean, but then
neither is he. We've both had our flings and are ready to
settle down.'

Recalling her conversations with Rick about Lucia,
Sancia thought he would not accept that point of view.
She had nothing in her past to which he could object, but
also, he was no longer interested in testing her virginity.

She could not conceal from Judy that hers was not a
normal marriage. When Rick came they occupied
separate bedrooms. She shrank from using her grandmother's, though the fourposter had been removed, and a
modern bed installed. Rick occupied it on his short visits
and had asked for a double one, saying he liked to have
plenty of room. He had accompanied this remark with a
sidelong look at her which caused her heart to increase its
beat, but had instantly resumed his most distant
expression as if he regretted an indiscretion. He was
always courteous, even kind, but he remained . . . aloof.
To Sancia the room was still haunted by the presence of
his arrogant grandparent with whom she continued to
identify him, Giovanni Antonelli, who had wanted to
marry her mother to a brute and a bully, if what Rick had
said was true. She took for her own use the smaller
bedroom next to it, which was so completely done over
that it bore no resemblance to its former appearance, and
the single divan did not remind her of what had occurred
within its four walls. She still regretted that she had been
prevented from achieving the consummation which
would have made her wholly Rick's, but she would tell
herself angrily that she was being idiotic. To Rick such

an experience was commonplace, and would have only cheapened her. As it was, she had the distinction of being the one woman he had desired and not possessed, though now that he owned the *palazzo*, desire had died.

Judy was puzzled by the situation. Rick had returned to Milan that morning, and as they sat by the fire, she asked, 'But if you want him, Sancie, and you do—I've seen how you look at him—why don't you make him want you? He did once.'

'He wanted what he could obtain through me,' Sancia said sadly. 'Don't probe, Judy. There was another woman, and I think there still is.'

'Yet when he was left the house, he married you?'

Sancia smiled bleakly. 'I think he felt bound to carry out Nonna's wishes. In some ways he's surprisingly scrupulous. Perhaps, for some reason, he couldn't marry the other woman.'

Judy said no more, realising that she had touched upon a sore subject. But then, she thought, Sancia had always been a fool when it came to managing the opposite sex. She was lovelier than ever, having developed a serene Madonna look that added to her beauty, and it was amazing that her husband could resist her. She must be frigid after all, Judy decided, and his passion must have repelled her. Men soon tired of unresponsive women— but why couldn't she pretend to reciprocate instead of looking so wistful? She would have been astonished to learn that they had never slept together. That, Sancia never told her.

In spite of Rick's disapproval, Sancia continued her solitary walks through the city's by-ways, usually at dusk, the hour she liked best. She loved the tortuous winding streets bisected by canals, the little arched bridges that crossed them, the *campos* in front of the big churches.

With Beppo to protect her she was confident she was in no danger, though as the days shortened and the tourists left there were often sinister figures lurking in dark passages.

Returning one evening as night was falling, she saw a shadowy figure wrapped in a black cloak standing by the door into the yard, gazing at the upstairs windows, and her heart missed a beat. A thief contemplating a break-in? She released Beppo from his leash and the dog approached, growling. Instantly the figure whipped round and tried to flee, but the dog had caught hold of the bottom of the cloak and was tugging at it. It fell to the ground, revealing a form clad in the universal jeans and sweater, and though the light was dim, Sancia could discern long black hair. The girl, for it was a girl, tried to rescue her cloak, screaming abuse at Beppo in the vernacular. He, thinking it was a lovely game, retained his hold of it. The girl kicked at him, and Sancia hastened to intervene.

'Don't kick my dog. Drop it, Beppo! Heel, boy!'

Beppo reluctantly relinquished his new toy, and the girl snatched it up and began to anxiously examine its folds for a tear.

'I don't think he's done any damage,' Sancia told her, for if the intruder was who she thought she was, she would understand English. 'If he has I'll pay for a new one, but you can't see out here. Won't you come in?'

The girl threw her a startled glance. '*Grazie, signora*, but I mustn't.' She continued to examine the cloak. 'This isn't mine,' she explained her anxiety, 'it's Suor Angelica's and she'll be furious if it's spoilt.'

'Then come where there is some light.' Sancia unlocked the door and it swung open. The girl stood hesitant, looking eagerly towards the house.

'*Il signor*? Is he at home?'

'No, he's in Milan.'

The girl gave a strangled sob. 'Then I go . . .'

'No, you don't.' Sancia seized her arm. It felt thin and brittle in her grasp. 'You're coming in. You're in trouble, aren't you? Perhaps I can help.'

For this was the young woman she had seen in the *campo*, she recognised her voice. Had Rick deserted her, or, terrible thought, was she pregnant? She had come to look for him, and seemed in distress. Sancia felt a hot wave of indignation on her behalf. Men!

'It's forbidden,' the girl said, hanging back.

'Who by? My husband? He isn't here. Come along.'

She guided her into the yard and shut and locked the door. A beam of light suddenly illuminated them. Bruno, Enrico's successor, was standing at the top of the steps. He was a short, grizzled individual whom Rick had engaged to drive the launch when Sancia wanted to use it and to act as guard, for the master considered old Luigi was not sufficient protection in his absence.

'*Signora, ch'é*? he called. '*Un vagabondo*?'

'*No un'amica*,' Sancia returned. A friend? Rick's mistress? But she was very curious about her guest.

Beppo following, Sancia conducted her visitor into the house and along the passages and stairs to the *salotto*, remembering with relief that Judy had gone to visit Enrico's family. She didn't want to have to explain the intruder to her, in fact she couldn't, not until she knew more herself. Her guest came willingly, glancing curiously about her. When they reached the *salotto*, she exclaimed, 'Oh, but it's beautiful!'

Dropping her cloak, she ran forward and knelt in front of the fire, holding out her chilled hands to its warmth.

'The convent is so bare and cold!'

Beppo, who had accepted her, came to sit beside her and she stroked his fur.

Seeing her for the first time in full light, Sancia stared at her visitor. The thin sweater outlined a slim, still immature body. Long black hair cascaded over her shoulders, the eyes she raised to Sancia's face were green, but she was a mere teenager, about thirteen or fourteen, Sancia judged. She could not be Rick's mistress, he would never seduce an adolescent, and from whom had she got the Rossini eyes? It was possible, of course, that the Rossinis had in their time left their mark on the population of Venice.

'We'll have some coffee,' she decided, pressing the bell. 'Won't you tell me your name?'

'Lucia . . .' the girl said, and Sancia started, 'Como— but that isn't a real name, it's that of a lake.'

'It could be a surname.'

A gleam of mischief showed in the green eyes. 'I guess I'm someone's by-blow.'

Good God, can she be Rick's daughter? Sancia wondered. It was possible, he had said he was about her age when he came back from college, which would be about the time this girl was conceived. Rick and Lucia? Oh, no, that would be too dreadful, and surely if that were so he would have acknowledged her, found some way to legitimise her? While she conjectured, Bianca brought in the coffee and this second Lucia sprang to her feet.

'Oh, how nice! You are being kind, *signora*.'

Bianca withdrew after giving Lucia a disdainful look.

Sancia opened a tin of biscuits which the visitor proceeded to share with Beppo. Though nearly as tall as her hostess, with the beginnings of a woman's shape, she behaved like an ingenuous child.

'You're living at a convent, did you say?' Sancia asked.

With her mouth full of chocolate biscuit, Lucia told her, 'The Convent of Santa Maddalena. It's a school really, though it's run by nuns.'

'Are you unhappy there?'

'Oh, it's all right. I have to be educated, *il signor* says. Term time isn't bad, but in the holidays when the other girls go home . . .'

Her eyes were bright with tears as she turned to look into the fire, and Sancia's warm heart went out to the pathetic waif. She knew what it was to long to be loved, and nuns weren't supposed to show affection, were they?

'I lived for *il signor*'s visits,' Lucia went on, 'but it's a long time since I've seen him. I thought he might be ill, that's why I came . . .' She brushed her tears away with the back of her hand. 'He said it would make no difference—but I'm forgetting, you're his wife, and you're lovely, like someone I knew when I was little. No wonder he's forgotten me.'

'I'm sure he hasn't, but he should have told me about you.' Why hadn't he, unless her horrid suspicion was true? But whether it was or wasn't, Sancia was sure this was her mother's child. Her sister—a wonderfully warming thought.

'I must ring up your convent,' she went on, 'they'll be worried about you.'

'Please don't,' cried Lucia, 'they'll send that horrid Suor Teresa to fetch me, who always pinches me. I was going to run away if I couldn't find *il signor*.

'My dear child, be sensible; when you're missing they'll go to the police, and that would not please *il signor*. You shall stay here tonight, and in the morning I'll take you back and talk to this Suor Teresa.'

Somewhat unwillingly, Lucia gave her the number.

Sancia asked to speak to the Principal, wondering if she ought to have said Mother Superior or whatever. After giving her name, she was put through to a surprisingly gentle voice enquiring her business. She seemed shocked when Sancia told her where Lucia was.

'To go there of all places! *Signora*, I do apologise. The naughty child shall be collected at once and suitably punished.'

'Please don't do that. It's late and I'll keep her until the morning when I'll come and see you.'

'*Signora*, you must not do that.' The woman was emphatic. 'It would not be wise. We do our best for our pupils, but Lucia has always been wayward and difficult; she should not be encouraged to be disobedient.'

'Do you know who she is?' Sancia demanded abruptly.

'*Si, signora*, but I must not say. I have promised.' There was a slight pause, and she went on, 'But to set your mind at rest, I may tell you this, she is not your husband's child.'

Sancia didn't doubt her word and felt a surge of relief, but if not Rick's daughter, she was certain she was her mother's.

'Thank you for that assurance. Then I may keep her tonight?'

'*Signora*, your husband would not approve.'

'You can leave him to me,' Sancia returned sweetly. 'Anyway, he's not here.'

After a few more expostulations, she was allowed to have her way, and she sped back into the *salotto* on winged feet, having used a connection elsewhere so Lucia should not overhear. Rick's interest in the girl was innocent and she suspected she had found him out in a greater and more generous action that what he had done for her.

When the master was absent, dinner was replaced by supper, eaten off a trolley by the fire. Under the influence of sympathy and good food, Lucia became expansive. She had spent her earliest years at an infants' home, where a beautiful lady, 'with hair like yours' used to visit her, but when she was old enough to board at the convent school, she ceased to come. *Il signor* did not desert her, and always remembered her on her name day and at Christmas, in spite of working so hard in Milan.

'We always spoke English together,' Lucia told her. 'As you must know, his mother was English, and he said the first words he spoke were English. Though he was very young when she died he missed her terribly. It was a bond that we were both orphans.'

Information that subtly wounded Sancia; there was so much about himself that Rick had never told her. Lucia knew about Nonna's bad heart, and said how worried Rick had been about her. He had wanted her to sell the *palazzo* and live in Milan, where he could watch over her, but she refused to budge. Adding to his responsibilities, demanding help and advice she wouldn't take, Sancia thought, and now it was revealed that Lucia Everard and her daughter had been another of his burdens.

'When he told me he was going to get married, I was sure I would lose him,' Lucia went on dolefully. 'Wives are so . . . so possessive, I . . . I cried, he hates that, but he did his best to comfort me.'

Sancia recalled that painful scene, but she didn't tell Lucia she had witnessed it. She asked, watching the girl's face, for if Lucia had formed a romantic attachment to Rick it would complicate the plan that was forming in her mind, 'You didn't dream he might marry you when you were grown up?'

Lucia stared at her with a shocked expression.

'Oh, no, no, *signora*! I never thought of that! I'd as soon dream of marrying St George or San Marco. Besides, he's so much older!' She returned her gaze to the fire. '*Il signor* is the only person I have belonging to me, though he doesn't really. I did dream he might be my father.'

Which, Sancia had been assured, he was not, but she was relieved to learn that Lucia's feeling for him was filial. As the top floor was in the process of redecoration, Sancia put Lucia into Rick's room and lent her a nylon nightdress, which delighted her. At the convent they wore calico, not because it was cheaper, but because it was less becoming. When she was settled, Sancia decided to ring Rick up. She only called the flat when some emergency cropped up, and she always dreaded hearing a female voice answer the phone. What she didn't know couldn't distress her, whatever her suspicions. But this time she had learned something to his credit.

It was getting late, but Rick never went to bed early, and for once she hoped to disconcert him. He was a little while answering the phone and she feared he was out, but eventually she heard the deep-toned voice which never failed to move her.

'*Pronto. Ecco Antonelli.*'

'Riccardo.' Lately she had taken to using his full name. 'It's Sancia.'

'Is something wrong?'

'Not exactly. I've had a little adventure.'

'*Cara mia*, what have you been doing?'

'Assisting a damsel in distress. Rick, why do you always try to conceal your good deeds?'

'What the devil are you talking about?' He sounded anxious.

'Something you should have told me long ago, but

you're so pig-headed and proud you wouldn't explain.' She drew a deep breath. 'Riccardo, I've met someone who I believe is my half-sister.'

He denied it vehemently, said she was making a ludicrous mistake, but she stuck to her conviction. She had heard his sharp intake of breath when she made her revelation.

'I know I'm right,' she insisted. 'She has the family's green eyes, and her early life was spent at an orphanage, hence mother's interest in such a place; besides, I feel akin to her. Oh, Rick, why couldn't you tell me instead of letting me get a wrong impression? I believed . . .'

'That I had a mistress,' he cut in. 'That child! You always were ready to think the worst of me.' There was an acid note in his voice.

'You always contrived to show yourself in a bad light,' she retorted, wondering if he understood that it was her mistake over Lucia that had caused her to try to break her engagement.

'Mercenary, brutal and deceitful?' he suggested.

'I'm beginning to get quite a different picture of you . . .'

Again he interrupted her. 'Indeed? How interesting,' he sounded sarcastic and went on to demand how she had come to encounter Lucia. She told him of the incident with Beppo.

'She was forbidden to come near the house,'

'But why, Riccardo? By rights it's her home.'

'I can't go into all that on the phone. What have you done with her?'

'At the moment she's in your bed.'

He laughed, then said sternly, 'Sancia, I would ask you not to interfere. I know best. She's happy at the convent, she might even have a vocation, it's the best thing that could happen to her.'

'That child won't ever want to be a nun.' Sancia was sure of that. 'If she told you she was happy it was to please you. She's not. She's yearning for love and affection, like I did, and she needs a real home and a family. What's more she's going to get it. I'll be a mother to her, since . . .' her voice dropped, 'I can't have a child of my own.'

'And whose fault is that?' he demanded.

'Yours entirely,' she told him, and rang off.

Judy had come in before Lucia retired and had been introduced to her, Sancia saying she was a little friend who had got lost.

When she had finished phoning, Judy asked, 'Have you adopted another waif and stray?' looking pointedly at Beppo.

'She's not, she's a . . . relation.'

'That so? I noticed a family likeness, but what is dear Riccardo going to say? He must have his reasons for concealing her.'

'Quite a lot, I expect, but for once I'm going to have *my* way. I imagine the concealment had to do with my grandmother. Rick tried to hide my mother's indiscretions from her, but she's gone, and anyway I think Riccardo was quite wrong. After the first shock, she would have loved the child.'

Sancia forgot that the first shock might have been disastrous. She was exhilarated: not only was Rick exonerated, but she had uncovered a side of his nature that she had not known existed. The granite façade had crumbled to reveal a humanity and generosity beneath the ruthless expediency his business demanded of him. In addition she had dared to defy him in this matter of the second Lucia and intended to continue to do so, but she did not think he would continue to oppose her. From what she had learned he must have a genuine affection for the orphan—hadn't she witnessed his tenderness when he had tried to comfort her, when she feared he would desert her? Once she had decided he was incapable of softer feelings, but he had been devoted to Nonna, and had aided and protected her unstable mother and her child, providing for the latter when Lucia had grown tired of her, for that, Sancia surmised, was what had happened.

He had given Sancia herself a luxurious home, asking no more of her than that she should run it for him, when she had had nowhere else to go, and yet she had tried to stifle her love for him, because she had believed he was unworthy. But all that could change, she would make amends for her misjudgment of him, she would give him anything, everything, if he wanted her. But did he? Had he become content with their semi-detached existence? He had pointed out that an annulment was a way out if either of them desired their freedom, and had been most careful not to be tempted into consummating their union so that that escape route would be closed.

Some of her elation faded. Rick was a passionate man. Had he found another attachment, and was it too late to attempt to make her marriage into a real one? Wasn't it more likely that he would ask for his freedom one day, so that he could have a proper home with a wife and family in his Milan flat? Lost opportunities, she thought sadly. Would kindly Fate give her another one, or must she accept that she could never win Rick's love?

Next morning she took a reluctant Lucia back to the Convent of Santa Maddalena, and was duly interviewed by its Principal. She found her to be a benign but worldly woman in spite of her nun's habit. More than one stain upon the family escutcheon had been entrusted to her care, and to her discretion, for which her school had been well paid. She firmly refused to reveal any more of Lucia's history, beyond the fact that someone paid her fees, for hers was not a charity school, she said proudly. She evaded Sancia's direct questions, though her shrewd eyes had noticed her likeness to her pupil. Lucia, she said, was going through the awkward period of adolescence, but it would pass. Was the signora wise to interest herself in the little one? She might make her even more unsettled and rebellious, and there were others to be consulted before she could grant access to her.

She meant Rick, of course.

'Oh, that will be all right,' Sancia said, more confidently than she felt. 'I know who you mean, and you'll have his permission within a few days, and in any case I don't think you can stop her from visiting me.'

'I didn't say her benefactor was a man,' objected the Principal, adding mildly, 'and there is a military punishment for disobedience—"confined to barracks", it is called.'

Sancia shuddered. 'That won't be necessary, I'm sure.' From what she had seen of it, the convent was very clean, but bare and austere, and she knew how Lucia's sensuous nature, so like her own, would revolt from it.

She parted from a tearful Lucia with many promises she hoped she would be able to fulfil, and wondered if she should contact Rick again or wait for him to turn up.

He came the next day, but he wasn't alone.

CHAPTER ELEVEN

'SIGNORINA MANCELLI,' Rick introduced her. 'Daughter of one of our directors.' The firm retained its original name, though Rick was the dynamo that ran it. 'She's our advertising manager, and a very efficient one.' He smiled at the blonde woman.

She was a fair Italian, as many of the northern ones are, and she was beautiful and chic. Her cord trousers and suede jacket were smart and perfectly tailored; her hair beautifully set, her make-up, down to her lacquered finger nails, immaculate. Sancia judged she was about Rick's age, perhaps a little older—her foundation didn't quite conceal faint lines about her eyes and mouth—but she was magnetic, assured and apparently single. Sancia's heart sank.

'Giulia is having a short break in *Venezia*,' Rick explained. 'So I gave her a lift. Will you ring for coffee, *mia cara*? We could do with some refreshment. Would you care to freshen up, Giulia? There's a cloakroom along here.'

He treated the visitor with the easy familiarity of long and close association. Fool, fool that she was, Sancia thought despairingly, of course there had to be a woman in Milan. Judy present and she caught her eye as she lifted the receiver of the house phone Rick had had installed, to ask Bianca for coffee. Her friend's dark eyes were full of speculation. She knew what she was thinking, it was what she had always dreaded to discover herself.

Rick came back, completely self-possessed. For all his casual clothes, cords and open shirt, he looked distinguished, and seemingly quite unaware that he had dealt Sancia a mortal blow. From his point of view, she had no cause for complaint; he had kept his part of their bargain faithfully and never sought her bed. He would feel justified in finding satisfaction elsewhere.

Giulia appeared to be that new phenomenon, the emancipated woman with a career and a lover. Sancia felt a spurt of anger: how dared the Antonellis condemn poor Lucia for seeking a similar freedom? But her mother had borne a love-child, and Miss Mancelli would never allow herself to be so burdened. Of the two, Sancia considered her mother was the better woman.

Giulia returned, having removed all traces of the crossing—not that there had been many—and Bianca brought the coffee. Judy was introduced and Rick handed round the cups. Giulia looked round the room with a critical eye.

'So this is the famous *palazzo* you've told me so much about, and which has cost you so much, *mio amico*. Is it worth it?'

'Don't you think so?'

She shrugged her elegant shoulders. 'Me, I am all for what is modern. These ancient monuments do not enthuse me.' Her English was good, if a little precise. 'Now your flat in Milano, that is marvellous, don't you think so, *signora*?'

She smiled with her lips but not her eyes as she looked at Sancia.

Unwilling to admit she had not yet seen it, Sancia said noncommittally, 'I suppose so.' And Rick grinned mockingly.

'Sancia's taste is the same as mine, she doesn't care for

plate-glass and chromium,' he told her.

'The very young are often drawn to the antique,' Giulia remarked, as if that were a juvenile error.

'Sancia's old enough to have developed discrimination,' Rick informed her.

Giulia made no response to that, but smiled superciliously as she sipped her black coffee—she took neither cream nor sugar out of regard for her figure, which was excellent. Instead she asked some question about the business, as if she wanted to show Sancia how much she was in his confidence, but Rick snubbed her.

'You're on holiday. We've left the office behind for a few days.'

'I can never wholly put it out of my mind,' she returned, to emphasise how dedicated she was to his interests.

'Then try to do so, or your vacation won't do you any good.'

He's being very discreet, Sancia thought a little scornfully, no favouritism in public, but in private, ah, what then?

When Giulia came to take her leave, she asked in a perfectly audible aside, 'Will you dine with me tonight, Riccardo?'

'Not if you're going to talk shop,' he told her.

She gave him an arch look. 'I think I can find other subjects.'

They went out of the room and Sancia did not know if he agreed or not. There were, of course, only water taxis to be had in Venice, and she wondered if he would offer to take Giulia to her destination, but apparently he did not, for he returned almost immediately. Judy made a vague excuse and left the *salotto*, leaving them together. The bland suavity had left Rick's face and manner and he looked menacing as he regarded his wife from under frowning brows. Once Sancia would have quailed, but now she had someone to fight for, she found he could no longer intimidate her.

'Now, Sancia, an explanation, please. The convent rang me yesterday. I can't have you disturbing Lucia.'

'She's disturbed already,' Sancia returned. 'Riccardo, you're not being fair to that child.'

'She's rather more than a child, and I've done my best for her. As you guessed, she is Lucia's daughter, and another of my problems.'

He sat down and sighed.

'And the father?'

'Lucia would never say.' He smiled grimly. 'Afraid I'd damage him, I imagine. She was more loyal to him than he was to her.'

'So she had some good points.'

'But misguided ones. You'd better hear the whole story. Your mother's lover took her to Switzerland, but when he found she was pregnant and she refused to have an abortion, he deserted her. She appealed to me for help and I made the necessary arrangements. We told Nonna she had gone into retreat,' his lip curled sardonically, 'to do penance for her sins. But your grandmother, after she'd recovered from her heart attack, wanted Lucia home. I didn't dare to tell her about the baby, in case she had another one, and Lucia refused to have the child adopted. She said she'd been deprived of you, and she wouldn't give up this one. So we installed the poor mite in a well-run orphanage where she could visit her while living at the *palazzo*. Luckily Nonna never found out.'

'But she would have loved the baby,' Sancia protested, 'once she got over the shock.'

'*If* she got over the shock. I dared not risk it.'

'But when she went to school, did Mother tire of visiting her?'

'When she was no longer an attractive doll to play with, she did, but in fairness to Lucia, she wasn't well herself. She developed symptoms of the illness of which eventually she died.'

'Poor Mother,' Sancia sighed. 'But you, Rick, you were good to the child.' She looked at him admiringly. Between them, all the Rossini women had been demanding, and she supposed she should include herself among them, but he had been their unfailing refuge and support at a time when he was deeply involved in his own concerns.

'I did what I could.'

'But now Lucia thinks you've deserted her.'

'She was becoming too intense,' he said shortly, 'it wasn't good for her. I hoped she'd find friends among the other girls, if I gradually faded out.'

Looking at him, so virile and handsome, so vividly alive, Sancia thought that to a young girl sequestered in a convent, he must have appeared like someone out of this world: St George the dragon slayer or St Mark, as Lucia had said.

'That would be rather cruel, Rick,' she told him. 'Her hero-worship is quite innocent, she thinks of you as a father figure.'

At which definition Rick did not look at all pleased, and she laughed.

'Of course she'll always adore you,' she added, 'and so she should.'

He glanced at her quizzically. 'A rather different attitude from yours,' he observed drily.

Sancia flushed. 'We were talking about Lucia. I want to have her to live with me.'

'That's impossible. There'd be talk. The Rossinis are an old and honourable family. I won't have Nonna's memory besmirched.'

'It won't be. People are much more tolerant nowadays, and only you and I know who she really is. Anyway, ancient lineage and family honour are out of date now. But Rick, why couldn't you have told me? Didn't you trust me? You know what I thought.'

Rick's face wore his most uncompromising expression and his eyes were glacial.

'You believed, on very flimsy evidence, that I was a cradle-snatcher and a seducer of teenagers, unworthy to touch your immaculate self.'

She flinched from his bitter tone. It must seem so to him, but she hadn't known Lucia was so young; she said uncertainly, 'You must admit appearances were against you.'

'And then you talk about trust.'

'Now you're being perverse!' she cried despairingly.

'Added to my other faults?'

He stood up, walked over to one of the mirrors and seemed engrossed in re-arranging the loose cravat he wore pushed into the collar of his shirt. Sancia could see his reflection and noticed that the hair on his temples was touched with silver. The heavy responsibilities he carried were leaving their mark. If only he would confide in her, let her help to ease them, but he shut himself away from her, had never told her much about his real self, reserving intimate converse for that supercilious blonde. His good deeds she had only discovered by accident.

Suddenly he swung round.

'As you say, the past died with Nonna. You and this girl are all who are left of the Rossinis. Do you really want to have her to live with you?'

'Oh, yes, please. I've never asked you for anything yet. All you've given me was unsolicited.'

'I tried to anticipate your wishes. Give you everything you could want.'

Everything except his love.

He went on, 'Very well. Have her if you wish, but she must continue with her education.'

'Thank you, thank you!' Sancia's eyes shone. 'Does that school she's at take day pupils?'

They discussed arrangements for Lucia, and Sancia realised that he had a fatherly affection for the girl, and was pleased by her interest in her. Could she become a bond between them? Then she remembered Signorina Mancelli.

'Are you going to dine with your colleague?' she asked.

Rick shook his head. 'I've enough of her in Milano. I'd prefer to take you out . . .' His eyes crinkled with laughter. 'For a change.'

An ambiguous statement. Had he sensed her suspicions about the other woman? His face revealed nothing, and she mustn't betray her jealousy, that would be fatal.

'I should like that. Will you ring the convent? I think the Principal suspected me of trying to abduct her pupil. Oh, she was the soul of discretion, she never mentioned your name.'

'So you went to see her? You're certainly persistent when you want something! First that mongrel hound, then this little girl—what next, I wonder?'

She raised luminous eyes to his in unspoken appeal, and saw his expression change, a sudden flame leap into his eyes.

'Sancia . . .' he began hoarsely.

Judy came rushing into the room.

'Beppo has bitten the postman! You'll have to do

something, Riccardo, if Sancia doesn't want her pet hauled off by the police.'

Rick placated Beppo's victim with a large sum of lire and a promise that it shouldn't occur again, which, he remarked sardonically, was actually only too probable. But the magic moment had passed and he had become remote again. Sancia wondered if she had imagined the light in his eyes and that emotional utterance of her name. Beppo chose his moments, she thought sadly, and never was one more inopportune.

But she had great hopes of the evening ahead. It was unusual for Rick to take her out; he preferred, when he came to the *palazzo*, to take his meals at home, or if he did go out he left her behind. She felt as excited as a girl on her first date. They were to go to Florian's, and Rick hired a water taxi to take them to *San Marco*. She selected a green brocade dress, princess style, that clung to her figure but flowed out round her feet, with gold accessories. Rick's diamond necklace was about her neck; he had given her that and also the diamonds in her ears. He had always been most generous. With it she wore a mink stole, another lavish gift.

Rick in evening dress was always a pleasure to behold. The severe black and white became him, the well-cut jacket emphasising the breadth of his shoulders, his trim waist and narrow flanks.

Unfortunately they had chosen the best-known restaurant in Venice. They hadn't been seated long at their table for two, when Sancia spotted Giulia Mancelli. She was with a prosperous-looking middle-aged man, a typical Italian, short and dark with a roving eye. Giulia was dressed discreetly in black silk and pearls, but her gown clung to her seductively although it had a high neck and long transparent sleeves. It wasn't long before she recognised them.

'Riccardo!' She came to them, swaying her hips. 'So you came out after all. I thought you said you were staying in, but perhaps your wife persuaded you to change your mind.' She shot Sancia an evil look. 'But since you are here, let's join forces.' Without waiting for Rick's consent, she called to a passing waiter.

'*Cameriere, una tavola per quattro, per piacere.*'

Rick gave Sancia a comical look and shrugged, but made no protest as the exchange was made. The other man—Adriano, Giulia introduced him—seemed as much a puppet as she was. Her evening completely spoiled, Sancia wondered if Rick wasn't secretly pleased by the encounter. He ordered an expensive meal, saying it was his treat, and still more expensive wine, and seemed amused by Giulia's obvious coquetry. It occurred to Sancia that if they were living together she was wasting a lot of effort, and that thought gave her some comfort, for Giulia wasn't the sort to exert herself for the already conquered.

Adriano, finding himself ignored by his lady, started to pay Sancia heavy compliments. Once he laid his pudgy fingers over her hand as it lay on the table. Sancia's instinct was to snub him and snatch it away, but, catching a black look from Rick, she let it lie. If he could flirt, so could she. She turned towards the stout gentleman and did her best to charm him. Apparently with success, for an avid look came into his eyes.

But it was not a comfortable evening.

They came out into the lighted square as the 'Moors' on top of the clock tower were striking ten, under a star-strewn sky.

'The night is still young,' Giulia cried. 'Riccardo, you

have your speedboat at the *palazzo*, have you not? Let's drop these two there and go for a spin on the lagoon. I am sure they won't mind. Sancia looks tired.'

But she had gone too far.

'You're on holiday,' Rick told her, 'but I'm not. I have to be up early in the morning and I need my sleep.'

'You sound as if you're getting old,' the disappointed Giulia snapped. She knew she was defeated.

Sancia heard his words with a heavy heart. Rick would be gone almost immediately. He had only paid a flying visit to dispose of Lucia. He had gone to the convent that afternoon. Lucia was to spend her half-holidays with Sancia, and next term she would become a day scholar, so there was nothing to stay for. Nothing had come of this evening. All was as it had been before, but not quite, for until that morning she had not known of the existence of Giulia Mancelli.

They parted to go their different ways, Giulia and her escort across the square, Rick and Sancia to the quay and the waiting taxi.

Adriano squeezed Sancia's hand as he shook it.

'*Bella signora*, I hope that we meet again.'

Not if I can help it, Sancia thought, but she smiled at him sweetly.

Rick said nothing during the short ride home, but as she ascended the stone steps to the upper regions, he suddenly gripped the nape of her neck.

'Did you have to encourage that greasy slob? I thought you were fastidious.'

'Rick!' she cried in alarm, as she teetered on her high heels. 'You'll have us both over backwards!'

He steadied her with his other hand and propelled her forward, along the entry and into the *salotto*. Judy was out and it was empty and dark. She stumbled against a piece of furniture as Rick said, 'There are limits to what a man can endure.'

'A trying situation for you,' Sancia concurred with false sweetness. 'When you do decide to take your wife out, she should have had more tact. Is she still your mistress, or is she ex?'

'Giulia has never been my mistress, and I don't care what *she* does.'

He touched the light switch and the chandeliers bloomed into scintillating cascades of light. Then she saw he was white with barely restrained passion.

'Sancia,' he went on harshly, 'I promised I'd never touch you, since you find me physically repellent, and I've kept my word at some cost to myself, but I'm damned if I'll stand for you carrying on with someone else.' He seized her by her shoulders and there was a red glare in his eyes. 'What do you get up to when I'm away? Are you your mother's daughter after all?'

The English half of him was entirely submerged in the primitive Latin male, and with rising exultation Sancia realised that he was madly jealous, which he wouldn't be if he were indifferent. His grip of her shoulders was very painful, there would be bruises, but she didn't care. At last he had ceased to be remote.

'And if I am?' she asked provocatively, her long green eyes alight with mischief. 'I've plenty of opportunity with you away.'

His hands were like iron clamps, as he returned tersely, 'If you're acting like a tart, I'll throttle you and then shoot myself!'

'Oh, Rick . . .' She was half laughing, half crying '. . . such melodrama . . .'

She got no further, as his control broke, and her own repressed feelings rose in spate to overwhelm her as his mouth closed over hers in a hard, punishing kiss. He swept her up in his arms and made for the bedroom, kicking the door shut behind him. There, in the dark, he stripped the beautiful brocade gown from her shoulders, wrenched the diamond necklace from her neck, his own expensive suit following them to the floor, as he tore it off. But Sancia felt no fear as he flung her across the bed. He wanted her desperately, that was clear, although he might be motivated by jealousy and rage, and she was filled with triumph. As he came down upon her, all her frustration, her hopeless longing, was swept away in one vast surge of eager response.

There was pain, but that was soon forgotten. Rick was making her his, the spectre of annulment banished for ever. Now there would be no going back. Sensation drowned all thought, her slight body locked against his lean hard one as they merged into one. After the frenzy was over, satiated, they slept, she lying in his arms, at last where she had yearned to be.

Sancia awoke to a new day, early sunlight showing through the slats of the blinds. Rick was sleeping quietly, one arm thrown possessively across her breasts, which were sore from the ravages of his lips and tongue. Carefully she disengaged herself and went into the bathroom to shower. There was a towelling wrap hanging on the door, which she used to cover her nakedness, and she went back to sit beside him on the bed, feasting her eyes upon his unconscious face and bare torso. His incredible eyelashes veiled his eyes, and lightly she stroked them, as—how long ago it seemed—she had wanted to do on the Lido beach. Her touch awoke him. He opened his eyes and looked up at her with such tender adoration that her heart seemed to melt in her breast.

Then recollection returned and he shot up into a sitting position.

'*Dio mio*, what have I done?'

Sancia laughed softly. 'You merely claimed your conjugal rights, darling.'

He groaned. 'I broke my word.'

'Thank God you did, otherwise I might never have known how much you wanted me.'

'Wanted you?' he exclaimed. 'It's been sheer hell keeping my distance! That's why I only dared to come here occasionally, but I acted like a brute last night, and you a virgin . . . but you provoked me.' He looked at her ruefully. 'I warned you not to do that.'

'Well, you produced that sexy bitch, and when she spoilt my evening, I tried to retaliate with that nasty oily creature.' She smiled tremulously. 'It seems to have worked.'

'Sancia, *amore mia*,' very gently he took her hands and drew her towards him. 'Believe me, there's never been any other woman for me since I met you. It seemed too good to be true that you were destined to be my bride. You had all poor Lucia's beauty but none of her frailty, but you were frozen, asleep, and I set to work to rouse you to life, and love . . . I thought I was succeeding, when you suddenly withdrew, wanted to break our engagement, and that made me mad. Afterwards, when you threw the wine in my face,' he grimaced, 'it seemed I had become abhorrent to you. But I couldn't let you go back to that dreary life in London, so I married you on your own terms, and tried to make you happy here.'

'You've been wonderful, Rick,' she said sincerely. 'But all along I thought it was the *palazzo* you wanted, and that . . . hurt.'

'Oh, damn the *palazzo*,' he exclaimed. 'Don't you

know I love you, the only woman I have ever loved or ever will.' He smiled as her eyes became luminous at this admission. 'Have I melted that little cold heart at last?'

Sancia raised her eyes to his, wondering if when heaven was reached it would be like this.

'You did that long ago, but I was a little scared of you at first, you seemed so important, and so . . . so ruthless. But now I know what you're really like, so generous and . . . noble, I love you more than ever.'

'Hold on, you're overdoing it.' He gave her his familiar mocking grin. 'Noble is a bit too much. I'm only a very ordinary man who has had a few difficult situations to deal with, and the good God gave me the strength to tackle them. You're not still scared of me, though I did behave like a beast last night?'

'Not in the least,' she told him, 'and if you hadn't been—er—provoked, we shouldn't be here now, like this.'

He drew her down until she lay with her head on his chest, and he wrapped his arms around her.

'This is bliss.'

'Amen to that.' She raised her face to meet his kiss.

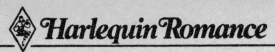 **Harlequin Romance**

Coming Next Month

2869 CARPENTARIA MOON Kerry Allyne
Photographer Eden arrives to be tourist director at an Australian
cattle station, asked by Alick, a friend, but finds the station is
owned by his older brother who regards her as the latest girlfriend
Alick is trying to dump!

2870 WINNER TAKE ALL Kate Denton
When a campaign manager recommends that her boss, a Louisiana
congressman, find a wife to dispel his playboy reputation, she
never thinks she'll be the one tying the knot!

2871 FORCE FIELD Jane Donnelly
For a young amateur actress, playing Rosalind in an open-air
production in Cornwall is enjoyable. But being emotionally torn
between the estate owner's two sons, a sculptor and an artist, is
distressing—until real love, as usual, settles the matter.

2872 THE EAGLE AND THE SUN Dana James
Jewelry designer Cass Elliott expects to enjoy a working holiday
until her boss's son unexpectedly accompanies her and their arrival
in Mexico proves untimely. She's excited by the instant rapport
between herself and their Mexican host, then she learns that Miguel
is already engaged....

2873 SHADOW FALL Rowan Kirby
Brought together by a young girl needing strong emotional
support, a London schoolteacher and the pupil's widowed father
fall in love. Then she learns of her resemblance to his deceased wife
and can't help wondering if she's just a substitute.

2874 OFF WITH THE OLD LOVE Betty Neels
All of Rachel's troubles about being engaged to a TV producer
who doesn't understand her nursing job and expects her to drop
everything for his fashionable social life are confided to the
comfortable Dutch surgeon, Radmer. Then, surprisingly, she finds
Radmer is the man she loves!

Available in November wherever paperback books are sold, or
through Harlequin Reader Service.

In the U.S.
901 Fuhrmann Blvd.
P.O. Box 1397
Buffalo, N.Y. 14240-1397

In Canada
P.O. Box 603
Fort Erie, Ontario
L2A 5X3

What readers say about Harlequin romance fiction...

"I absolutely adore Harlequin romances!
They are fun and relaxing to read, and
each book provides a wonderful escape."
—N.E.,* Pacific Palisades, California

"Harlequin is the best in romantic reading."
—K.G.,* Philadelphia, Pennsylvania

"Harlequins have been my passport to the
world. I have been many places without
ever leaving my doorstep."
—P.Z.,* Belvedere, Illinois

"My praise for the warmth and adventure
your books bring into my life."
—D.F.,*Hicksville, New York

"A pleasant way to relax after a busy day."
—P.W.,* Rector, Arkansas

*Names available on request.

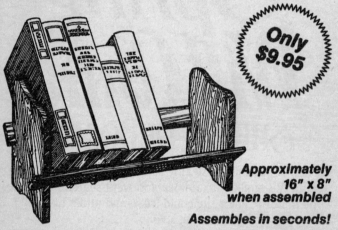

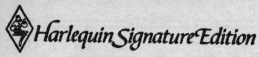

Penny Jordan

Stronger Than Yearning

He was the man of her dreams!

The same dark hair, the same mocking eyes; it was as if the Regency rake of the portrait, the seducer of Jenna's dream, had come to life. Jenna, believing the last of the Deverils dead, was determined to buy the great old Yorkshire Hall—to claim it for her daughter, Lucy, and put to rest some of the painful memories of Lucy's birth. She had no way of knowing that a direct descendant of the black sheep Deveril even existed—or that James Allingham and his own powerful yearnings would disrupt her plan entirely.

Penny Jordan's first Harlequin Signature Edition *Love's Choices* was an outstanding success. Penny Jordan has written more than 40 best-selling titles—more than 4 million copies sold.

Now, be sure to buy her latest bestseller, *Stronger Than Yearning*. Available wherever paperbacks are sold—in October.

**A chilling new mystery by
Andrew Neiderman**

ILLUSION

They were madly in love.
But suddenly he disappeared without a trace.
Confused and disappointed, she began to ask
questions . . .

Only to discover that her lover had actually been dead for
five years.